# MURDER iN MIDWINTER

## FLEUR HITCHCOCK

D0062796

*For Ruby*

First published in the UK in 2016 by Nosy Crow Ltd
The Crow's Nest, 10a Lant Street
London, SE1 1QR, UK

Nosy Crow and associated logos are trademarks and/or registered
trademarks of Nosy Crow Ltd

Text © Fleur Hitchcock, 2016
Cover illustration © Robert Ball, 2016

A CIP catalogue record for this book is available from the British Library

Printed and bound in the UK by Clays Ltd, St Ives Plc
Typeset by Tiger Media

Papers used by Nosy Crow are made from wood grown in sustainable forests.

ISBN: 978 0 85763 638 6

www.nosycrow.com

# Chapter 1

The bus stops for the millionth time and I look down at my phone for the millionth time.

A little envelope appears in the corner of the screen. I click on it.

It's my sister, Zahra.

*What you gonna wear to the party?*

Staring out of the window at the thousands of people stumbling along the pavement I imagine my wardrobe, mentally discarding clothes that I can't possibly wear to the end-of-term party: too cheap, too old, too "princessy".

My green dress? Just right. Not sure about shoes

though…

*Dunno. You?* I text back.

*Dunno*, she replies. The bus creeps forward. There's a long pause from Zahra.

My phone buzzes again.

*Can I borrow your black jacket* ☺ ☺ ☺ ?

We judder to a halt. There are even more shoppers now, in layers. The ones nearest the bus fall on and off the kerb, jamming along faster than those in the middle who struggle past each other, pulling their shopping close, their faces grey under the street lights.

☺ *In x change for purple platforms* ☺ I type.

I press send and a huge woman comes and lands her enormous bottom on the seat next to me. She's got a ton of shopping and she's too hot and I can see a bead of sweat trickling down her skin just in front of her ear. She's damp. Hot and damp.

She glances at me, and then looks away. Then looks back again.

"Unusual that," she says.

"What?"

"Mallen streak, it's called, isn't it?" She puts her hand up to her hair. "The white bit."

I nod. I know it's unusual, but I like it. It makes

us special, me and Zahra and Dad. Black hair, white streak. Hereditary. Like skunks, or Cruella de Vil.

The bus makes a dash over a set of lights and I find myself staring at a new set of shoppers. We head towards one of the huge Christmas window displays and I get my phone on to the camera setting so that I can take a picture for Zahra. It's difficult to get a decent shot, there are so many people in the way, but I hold it up ready to click. We judder to a halt and I start taking photos even though the windows are slightly further ahead.

*Click*

*Flash*

*Click*

*Flash*

*Click*

*Click*

What was that?

*Click*

Looking through the viewfinder, I see a man. He's in a gap in the crowd. He's tall, with curly hair. Ginger hair, I think. Everyone else seems to be rushing past him but I notice him because he's standing still. There's a woman there, she's still too. They're arguing. He disappears as the crowd swirls around him. A couple with shopping bags swing across the view, some kids, a large family, but my eye goes back to the man the moment he reappears.

*Click*

*Click*

He's holding something.

*Click*

Is that a gun? He's drawn a gun on her?

I keep taking the photos, and the flash goes off half the time and then the man looks at me and so does she. I take another photo and he runs and the bus pulls away, stop-starting through the crowds all the way down to Piccadilly Circus.

I stare back up the pavement but I can't even see the lights of the department store now. The woman next to me gets off, and a bloke reading a book gets on. It's all really normal, but what have I just seen?

Was that a gun or not?

I flick through the photos.

There are quite a few where the flash just reflects on the window, one really good one of the window display, and then three blurry pics of the man and the woman. Two from the side, one straight on, looking right at me. I zoom in on his hand.

Definitely a gun. Or definitely the barrel of a gun.

A man holding a gun? In Regent Street, ten days before Christmas.

The time on the photo is 17.14. It's only 17.26.

I swallow, feel sick, excited then terrified. I doubt myself.

But he *did* have a gun. I've seen enough movies to know that's what he was holding.

The bus swings down towards Trafalgar Square. People pile on and off and I look at the pictures again. I text Zahra.

*I've just seen something really weird – scary.*

*What?*

*A man with a gun on the street.*

I look around on the bus to see if there's a policeman. Or should I jump off and look for one on the street?

*Whaaat? Are you OK?*

*Yes – I'm OK.* I type, but my hand shakes and the phone shakes with it.

*Come home,* says Zahra.

Waterloo Bridge whizzes by and I jump off at my stop and wait, shivering, for the next bus to take me home.

# Chapter 2

The huge windows of our shop illuminate the pavement and light up the underside of the railway bridge that crosses the road. This time of year, it's all made brighter by a host of random flashing Christmas lights that Dad's wrapped around everything possible. The really posh bath in the window manages to look utterly bargain basement, festooned with tiny glowing Santas, and he's jammed the matching £600 toilet with miniature reindeer lamps. It's all going on and off all over the place, but it makes the shop look warm and welcoming, even more warm and welcoming than it does normally.

.I rush in, desperate to talk to Zahra. She'll be upstairs, but I have to pick my way through the shop to get there.

Azil's in the showroom, discussing copper piping with a man in overalls, and Mum's trying to persuade a woman that the cream bathroom suite that's been in the middle of the shop for two years would look brilliant in her new loft conversion. It's so normal in here it feels unreal.

Granddad comes through from the kitchenette. I could tell him?

"Granddad," I say.

He's behind the till now. He holds up a finger and points to the phone.

"Just a sec, Maya darlin'," he says. "Yes, Michael, seventy quid each — but I can do them at sixty-five if you take all three? What about it?" He pauses, his finger still held up to keep me silent. "Yes, so Tuesday? Cutting it fine but they should be here by then ... well sixty each OK, but you're breaking my heart, Michael, you know that..."

Granddad listens, his head nodding, as he scribbles something on the corner of an envelope before tapping an order into the computer.

I can see he's going to be more than a minute so I squeeze past a pregnant woman, who's admiring a mirror that plays three radio stations, and push through a stack of cardboard into the kitchenette.

The twins are sitting on the floor peeling coloured wrappers from a giant tin of Quality Street.

"My," cries Ishan.

"My," echoes Precious.

Precious offers me a naked toffee, spreading the yellow wrapper over her eye and staring at me through it.

"Thank you, Precious," I say. "But d'you know, I think I'll pass this time."

"Maya!"

I look up towards the door that leads up to our flat. It's Zahra. She looks exactly like I did two years ago. Same black hair, same streak of white front to back.

"What happened?" She takes the toffee off Precious and jams it in her mouth.

"I just saw him."

"Was he threatening anyone?"

"Well yes, this woman ... I've got a picture here, somewhere." I pull out my phone and click through the images. "Look."

Zahra peers over my shoulder. "What am I looking at?"

"There," I say, expanding the image to show the glint between the two black coats.

We stare at each other. Her black eyes looking back at mine. Reading each other's thoughts.

"Tell Mum," she says in the end.

I stick my head back past the cardboard into the shop. Mum's on her own with a box of toilet joints. "Twelve, thirteen, fourteen," she counts, dropping them into a wire basket.

"Mum," I say. "Can you talk?"

"Course, fifteen, sixteen, seventeen." She folds over the top of the box. "What is it?"

I look around at the aimless customers lifting up toilet seats and turning display taps. "Can I tell you upstairs?"

Mum's face goes from unconcerned to concerned in a millisecond. "What is it? What's happened?" She bustles behind me, shoving me past the cardboard, around the twins and up the stairs until we burst into our flat. "Tell me," she says, flumping into an armchair and giving me all of her attention. "What's happened?"

"I want to ring the police," I say.

"What? Why?"

I show Mum the picture. It takes ages to load. It's a rubbish reject phone of Dad's, but it's still a smartphone.

Her mouth drops open. "Is that what I think it is?" she says, reaching for Granddad's extra-strong specs. "Blimey," she says looking up at me. "What happened next?"

"The bus went on, and I left them behind."

Mum puts my phone on the table and stares out of the window into the flats behind.

The twins scrabble up the stairs and thump off to their room.

"Well," says Mum, "you'd better use the landline."

\* \* \*

"Hello? Police please." I've never rung the emergency services before, and it makes my heart go poundy. "I want to report something I saw earlier."

The woman on the other end is in a call centre full of noise that I can hear in the background. Someone near her says: "The ambulance is nearly with you." And I wonder whether I've rung the right number.

"Are you in danger?" asks my operator.

"No, I'm at home, safe."

"Can you give me your address?"

I give her my address, tell her I'm fine, but try to explain what I saw. "He had a gun."

"How old are you?"

"Thirteen – why?"

"Can you get an adult to make this call?"

"No – because I was the one that saw it."

There's a pause.

"What time was this?" asks the operator. I check my phone. "About quarter past five."

"Thank you caller, I'm transferring you."

So I run through the whole thing again. And I'm transferred again. And I stop feeling panicky and begin to feel somehow stupid and actually cross. By the third transfer I'm sitting cross-legged on the floor, pinging the elastic on my tights but I don't put the phone down because that would be giving up.

"Yes," I say when I finally get through to someone who listens. "I saw a man with a gun in Regent Street."

"And you recorded this?"

"Yes, sort of, on my phone."

"What time?"

I don't need to check again. "Quarter past five," I say.

"We'll send someone just as soon as we can," they say, and I put down the phone hoping very much that I've been taken seriously.

# Chapter 3

I hold up my hand. It's still shaking.

"Thing is, Granddad, I don't think I've ever seen a gun before. I mean a *real* one."

Granddad nods. He's listening to me, I can tell — but he doesn't answer. Instead, he reaches into a cupboard and pulls out an oily cardboard box. "Let's do a bit of work on the old motorbike, take your mind off it while we're waiting." He hands me a pot marked *valve paste* and a mushroom-shaped piece of metal. I take a blob of the paste and rub it gently into the metal, smoothing away the old carbon. I could use a drill to do this, but I prefer doing it by hand.

"Nothing like really good craftsmanship," he says, laying the pieces out on the kitchen table. "Don't make them like this any more. Keep going forever this will, when we've got it fixed."

He's right, doing this is comforting. It's something I've done a thousand times before, while listening to the football on the radio with Granddad or talking to the family, or outside on the balcony in the summer.

"Feeling better, sweetheart?" he says after a couple of minutes. He's peering at an ancient manual over his wonky reading glasses.

"It was scary, Granddad."

"I'm sure it was, love. But, you've done the right thing, calling the police."

The twins run through the kitchen, scattering Lego across the floor. They crash into the table, giggling, and run back the other way.

"Get out of it, you two," says Mum, driving them into the lounge.

I glance at the old electric clock on the wall. Fifteen minutes since I rang.

"What's going on?" asks Dad, struggling through the door with a stack of pizza boxes. "Why are you all looking so worried?"

* * *

It takes the police forty-four minutes. Two men in uniform arrive, take off their hats, sag on to chairs and clutch gratefully at Granddad's treacly cups of tea. They both look like people who have been on duty since early morning and would like to go home. But they do take me seriously.

"I saw a man pull a gun on a woman in the middle of town, with like, loads of shoppers all around them," I blurt. "From the bus."

The policemen look surprised and I make myself breathe slowly. I've obviously said too much too quickly but Zahra chooses that moment to pour a load of popping corn into a pan full of hot oil and the little explosions that follow fill the empty space, giving the policemen a chance to catch up and me a chance to be ordinary.

I stuff my hands under my armpits to stop them from shaking, and stretch a smile over my face.

"So, Maya, first things first – who was on the bus – you or him? And which bus?" says the tall one, looking at the bike-engine parts spread all over the table.

"I was on the 139, in Regent Street."

He fumbles for a pen and starts writing.

"And … what, in your own words, did you see?" he asks, his eyes flick from the paper to the box of motorbike parts.

I run through it all again. "A tall man, holding a gun, pointing it at a woman, on the street. Regent Street, at more or less exactly five fourteen. I took a photo, it's on my phone."

"Can we see?" says the short one.

"Yes – it's just here," I peer round the boxes and Granddad moves them to look underneath.

"I saw it earlier," he says.

"Is that an old Ducati?" The policeman asks Dad, who's sorting through the pizza boxes in case the phone's got caught inside.

Dad blinks at the question. "The bike? No idea," he says. "Ask her," he points to me.

"No," I say. "It's a Vincent."

Moving the fruit bowl and some cereal packets, I check the worktop, while Mum scans the dresser and Zahra stops making popcorn to look on the floor under the cupboards. The policemen stand and examine the chairs and stare at the clock, as if the phone might materialise there.

"It was here a moment ago – I showed the

pictures to Mum," I say, feeling desperate and stupid. "It can't be that difficult to find. It's got this pink cracked case." I don't tell them that the case falls off all the time and that all the pieces inside go flying all over the place.

"Have another look under this lot," says Granddad and the policemen join in, picking through the boxes and scrabbling on the floor.

"It'll be the twins," says Mum, sighing. "Ishan!" she shouts down the corridor. "Precious!"

The twins waddle into the kitchen. "Have you seen my phone?" I ask.

Precious shakes her head and looks at the floor. Ishan swings from foot to foot, looks at me sideways before he runs out of the room and Mum follows.

"NO!" I hear her shout and race to see what she's found.

The pink case is in the bathroom doorway. The battery's lying on the bath mat, the phone too. The screen's cracked but the first thing I really notice is the memory card.

"It's gone," I say. "The memory card's gone."

The short policeman appears behind me. "Is that important?"

I nod, blinking back tears and glaring at the

twins, who yelp and run away. "Yes, I changed the settings so all the pictures get saved to the card."

"Stick it all back in the phone anyway," says Mum, already on her hands and knees, peering down the cracks in the floorboards. "Just in case…"

"I'll talk to the twins," says Zahra. "See if they can tell me what they did with it."

"Let me see if anything's been reported, although I think we'd know by now," says the tall policeman, thumping back towards the kitchen, pressing the buttons on his phone as he goes.

He says something muffled and then I hear him say: "Five fourteen … Regent Street … just verify will you?"

I sniff back a tear and struggle to get the battery working in the phone. Slowly it switches on, pinging and swirling into life, and tells me that there's no memory card. I press the gallery icon and there are no pictures.

"Sorry," I say. "Nothing…"

The tall policeman smiles. He looks very tired. "Never mind. While your memory's fresh, tell us what you saw. Tell us *who* you saw."

They put down their mugs, pick up their pens, and write…

# Chapter 4

When they've gone, we watch a Spider-Man film on the telly. All of us together. I sit between Mum and Dad, and Granddad snoozes in the corner. Rain taps on the windows, and I get up every now and again to check the street below. It's empty.

The twins graze, passing through, grabbing handfuls of Zahra's popcorn, before scuttling off to fight over the Lego.

Mum keeps jumping up to search in places where the twins might have hidden the memory card, but it's so small, we'll never find it.

I don't really watch the film. No one in the

family's said anything, but I know we're all feeling unsettled.

Zahra goes to bed. I go to bed.

I hear Mum and Dad locking up, Granddad coughing his way up to the attic.

I pull back the bedroom curtain and look out on to the street again. Two figures stand in the shadows under the bridge. Is that unusual?

A shiver goes down my spine.

"Zahra?" I whisper. "You still awake?"

"Yes," she says.

"Can we share?"

"Yes." And I clamber out of my bed and snuggle in alongside her. She feels much warmer than I do. We fold into each other, me behind, her in front, which means that I have a warm chest and she has a warm bum. She holds her funny old rabbit, the one Dad bought on the day she was born, so he's warmest of all.

"How are you?" she asks.

"OK," I lie.

"You're not, are you?"

I lie there, feeling her warmth. It's like cuddling a huge teddy bear. I don't answer for a long time. I think about what I saw: a gun, a woman frightened and angry. The red-haired man. The camera flash. Them looking back at me. "If you want to know, I'm scared."

"You don't need to be. You saw him but why would he have seen you?"

"The camera flash. They looked up. He looked right at me."

"Oh!" she says, pulling me tighter.

We lie there listening to the trains thundering over the railway bridge, the endless helicopters circling overhead.

"Can I sing you our song?" she says, eventually. "For the Christmas concert?"

\* \* \*

I go through school the next day feeling jangly, but everything's really normal. We're doing *Romeo and Juliet* and we've just got to the death bit. Half the class is in tears, the rest are balancing pencils on their noses.

"So when Romeo sees Juliet, apparently dead—"

A cascade of pencils hits the floor.

Mr Nankivell pauses, and sighs. "What is it, Nathan?"

"What time are we doing the Secret Santa – Sir? Only I've got football practice and I don't want to be late."

"Just – let me get to the end – so Romeo says: '*O true apothecary! Thy drugs are quick. Thus with a kiss I die*', priming the audience for..." Mr Nankivell stops and stares at Nathan who has slung his bag over his back and is trying to sneak out of the classroom unseen.

There's a pause. Nathan freezes. We all stare.

Mr Nankivell sighs. "I give up," he says, and thirty chairs scrape across the floor. The entire classroom stampedes past him and I see that Zahra's making signs at me from the doorway. As I half stand to wave at her, the bell rings.

"So what do you think?" she asks me, waving toxic purple fingernails under my nose.

"Great," I say. "Brilliant, are those allowed?"

She ignores that. "And I've found sick yellow tights online. You know, that half shade between green and yellow, almost lime – and the shoes, you should see the shoes, Maya – well, you will see the shoes, they're so cute."

"Good," I say.

"You don't care, do you?" she says. "You're still thinking about last night, aren't you?"

"What if he killed her?" I say, and she hugs me.

*  *  *

Later, I walk back home with her and together we veer on to the South Bank. We're quickly caught in the bustle of people coming and going along the river, and like them, stop to stare at the coloured lights of the bridges and the Tate Modern warming up the freezing London dusk. A few leaves crunch under the thousands of feet and the smell of roasting nuts catches in my throat. The near horizon is a perfect pale green pierced by a single star, and the dome of St Paul's Cathedral shows as a lit silhouette against it.

"God, London's beautiful," says Zahra.

"Yes," I say. My mind is miles away, playing and replaying the scene from yesterday, all the way up to the police visit. The pictureless police visit.

"When we get home I'm going to search the twins' room," I say.

"Again?" she says.

Throwing our school bags to the ground we sit on a bench by the Globe and watch a small crowd form against the river railings. They're pointing at something below them, but I don't care, I'm too unsettled.

A man with a briefcase sits next to me and pulls

out a newspaper.

Zahra and I watch a police boat buzzing up the river towards us.

The police boat is joined by another police boat. They're still racing in our direction.

A toddler lets go of a balloon and howls as it takes off into the indigo sky. Her mother laughs and drags her off along the pavement.

The man leans forward to tie his shoelace.

A siren goes off behind us and an ambulance pulls around on to the cobbles in front of the Globe, closely followed by a police car. We stay on our bench and watch the ambulance crew and the policemen struggle over the railings and disappear.

"This looks too interesting – I've got to take a look," says Zahra.

Reluctantly, I leave the bench and follow her to the railings. The two police boats are tied up at the jetty. Below us, on the little beach, there are several people standing in a ring around something on the sand. There's a man in a white cover-all suit, several policemen and a paramedic. They're all staring down.

"'S'a body," says Zahra.

I peer at the darkened shore. People with reflective

strips on their clothes catch the light from mobile phone cameras and police torches.

"My husband spotted it," says a woman with pride.

"Yes," says her husband. "I did."

I tilt my head and realise that the thing I thought was seaweed is actually a pair of shoes. I trace my way up the body, slowly, just in case I see something horrible, but I can't see the head, until one of the policemen gets out of the way.

The beam of a torch flashes across the hair. Ginger. Ginger curls.

"Oh my God!" I mutter. "It's him. The man I saw from the bus."

# Chapter 5

But it isn't.

"Have a cup of tea," says Granddad. "How was school?"

I know he's trying to change the subject.

"I'm still not convinced it wasn't him," says Zahra, as she reaches into the bread bin with one hand and the fridge with the other.

"It wasn't," I say. "Definitely not."

"People look different when they're dead," says Granddad.

"Not *that* different," I say. "Wrong-shaped face, wrong nose. The man on the beach was skinny.

26

The man on the street was solid." My voice sounds cheery and matter-of-fact, but I don't really feel like that inside. I've never seen a dead body before. It was weird. Waxy.

"Just a coincidence, then," says Zahra. "You know, two red-headed men in a city of eight million."

Granddad takes my hand, and although he's really talking to Zahra, he looks at me as he says it. "There's no such thing as coincidence. If there's a damp patch on your ceiling and a puddle on your floor, then they're probably connected. Unless you've got a puppy of course." He laughs a rattly, smog-filled cough and struggles to the sink for a glass of water, then, having drunk three he flings himself back into the chair and pats me on the back of the head.

"How's the motorbike going?" asks Zahra. Now *she's* trying to change the subject – she never usually wants to know anything about the bikes. She hates machines. Unless they make milkshakes.

"I wonder who he is?" I ask. "The dead bloke."

"Go on," says Zahra. "You're dying to check." She stuffs the side of an enormous Nutella sandwich into her mouth.

We have a rule in our house about phones at the

table, but we're not really eating, it's only Zahra stuffing her gob. I enter the words: *Body, Thames beach, Globe*, and then narrow the search terms to the last twenty-four hours. It's there.

*Body pulled from Thames.*

And that's all there is.

I walk to the window and peer out into the darkness. Masses of people are on the street. Some moving, some still. Any of them could be him.

"Can we buy a Christmas tree yet, Granddad?" asks Zahra, licking chocolate off her fingers. "Only they're selling really good ones at the back of the market."

\* \* \*

On our way home from school the next day a man and a woman hand out newspapers at the underground station. I take one for Granddad.

"Thanks," I say and stare down at the headline.

There on the front page, is my man. The man I saw in Regent Street.

Even Zahra stops.

Without saying a word we take the paper to the side of the pavement and spread it across the back of a bench.

*MURDER SUSPECT PETER ROMERO*

*Police are advising the public that Peter Romero is considered dangerous. He is wanted in connection with the murder of Georgio Romero, art dealer ... (cont. p2).*

I read it over and over. The headline fragments in front of me. MURDER?

MURDER?!

Zahra reaches for page two. I think I've guessed what it might say before she even flicks it over.

*... who was yesterday found on the Thames shoreline in full view of thousands of tourists visiting the historic Globe Theatre. Post-mortem results show that he was shot and already dead before entering the water. Police are appealing for witnesses.*

My eyes leap down the page.

*Georgio Romero, 45, was born in Glasgow. After attending Manchester University, he went on to become an art historian, working closely with the National Gallery in acquisition and restoration. He was known as an international art dealer of significance.*

*Police say they would like to hear from anyone with any information about Georgio Romero's death, but that they are actively seeking the apprehension of his brother, Peter. They warn the public not to approach the suspect as he is considered dangerous.*

That's it.

I swallow hard and stare at the people pouring in and out of the underground station. There are thousands of them. The red-headed man could appear at any second. Zahra goes on reading and rereading.

Murder?

"Right." I grab Zahra by the elbow. "Time we got ourselves home."

"What are you going to do?" She jams the newspaper in her bag.

"I'm going to get you into the flat and I'm going to ring the police again," I say, rushing ahead.

"But you didn't actually see anything."

"I know, but I took a photo, with a flash." I duck around a street lamp, shouting back to Zahra on the pavement behind me. "He saw me. Black hair with a white streak."

She puts her hand up to her head. Her own streak glows yellow under the street light.

"I mean," I say, pulling her past a barrier. "How many of us are there?"

# Chapter 6

When we reach the flat I make the phone call again. This time I get through really quickly.

"The man in the paper, Peter Romero, he's the man I saw in Regent Street, with a gun."

The line clicks, and hums and after a few minutes I get a woman who introduces herself as Detective Sergeant Parker. She listens as I tell her what I saw in the street.

"You're absolutely sure it was him?"

"Yes – I know I don't have the photos, but it was him."

"And you actually saw him holding the gun?" she

asks.

"Yes," I say.

"And he saw you because the camera flashed?"

"Yes. And I'm scared he's going to find me," I whisper.

"Don't worry, Maya. London's a big place."

"I've got very obvious hair, and I was wearing school uniform, he might find me that way."

There's a long pause. "I understand," she says. "In the meantime, see if you can find that missing memory card – it would be really helpful."

\* \* \*

In the morning both Zahra and I wear bobble hats to cover our white streaks and soon we're in a crowd of school kids all heading the same way, all wearing the same uniform.

We stop at a pedestrian crossing. Every man I pass looks like Peter Romero. The one who looks most like him is a bloke with a beanie and a fluorescent jacket on the other side of the road. He stares at us all as we cross. I see him again on the corner of Union Street. I swear that he sees me, but a lorry load of roof tiles cuts us off from each other and Zahra and her friend Lou grab me by the elbows and sweep me on towards school.

I struggle through physics and Spanish, my brain clicking over and at break I hide in the toilets and ring the police number I rang last night.

"Yes – can I speak to Detective Sergeant Parker? I think I've seen Peter Romero again."

I have to stick my finger in my ear to hear over the babble of people applying make-up outside my cubicle.

The familiar voice comes on the line. "Where?"

"Union Street, Southwark – he was wearing one of those high-vis jackets. Next to a hole in the road. Less than an hour ago."

"We'll send a car to pick you up from school. Detective Constable Fallon will come to the school reception and accompany you home. Don't leave the building until he arrives. OK?"

\* \* \*

There should be a word for a mixture of fear and worry. I'd call it "feary". I am currently feeling feary. After maths, I rush to reception and find the detective reading the school magazine.

"Maya?" he says.

I nod.

"Just you?" he asks.

"Yes – my sister's staying for the Christmas

concert and she's in the choir."

She's with her friends, but I'd like to keep her with me. I'd like to go around with a big bubble protecting all my family and all my friends from that man out there.

"Put your hat on," the detective says, and we run for the police car parked on the zigzag lines outside the school. It only takes a moment to get me home.

\* \* \*

"Where's Zahra?" asks Mum. It's the evening and we're sitting at the back of the packed school hall. All the parents in the world seem to have crammed themselves inside.

"On stage?" I guess.

"Well the others are — but I can't see her," says Mum, half-standing.

"What d'you mean?" says Dad, picking something sticky from Ishan's hair.

"The others are up there but there's no sign of Zahra," says Mum. "She never said anything about doing anything special. I thought she was just singing in the chorus. It's just that if she's got a solo or something then we'll have to do something with the twins — they'll never sit here for longer than half an hour."

I look over all the people's heads towards the stage. I scan slowly left to right and then right to left. "I'll go and check out what's happening," I say.

"Good girl," says Granddad, snorting into a large white-cotton handkerchief and buffing it across the bottom of his nose.

I slip down the side of the hall to the corner of the stage. There's a girl with plaits that I recognise from Zahra's year.

"Is my sister here?" I ask.

She looks along the row. "She should be. Everyone else is – hey!" she nudges her neighbour. "Is Zahra here?"

There's shuffling while everyone checks to see who's there. "No," calls someone further along. "She went to the toilet about twenty minutes ago. I don't think she came back."

"She better get here soon," says someone else. "We're due to start at seven."

Something chimes in my head. A tiny alarm bell.

"Which toilets?" I ask.

Their heads bob forward as they all look at each other. "The ones by reception," calls a girl from the other end. "I think."

I check behind the green curtains at the back

of the stage, in case she's there frozen with stage fright. But she isn't. I knew she wouldn't be.

Feeling both calm and terrified, I ask Mrs Roxburgh the music teacher if she's seen Zahra.

"No, Maya," she says, tapping her watch. "I haven't, but she'd better get a move on."

The audience is still filing into seats, and there's five minutes before the concert is actually due to start so I duck out into the corridor. A clutch of sixth-formers are chatting and twiddling with their instruments. Normally I'd be a little shy of them, but this is an emergency.

"Have you seen Zahra?" I ask. "My sister, looks like me but—"

"Smaller?" asks a boy with hair like a nest. "No – not here."

I mumble thanks and charge down the passage that leads behind the hall. The doors at the end are locked. She can't be through there, so I turn back and blunder into the sixth-formers again. As I bust them apart they make exaggerated noises, and I hear someone tapping a microphone in the hall. Half running, half walking I get to reception, which is more or less empty.

Two Year Sevens are clearing up Coke cans.

The deputy head, Mr France, is talking to Tiggy Spence's mum, and the front doors into the car park are closed. Outside is the police car that brought us here.

I hover quite close to Mr France, but not too close, trying not to look like I'm listening to their conversation, but they're talking about something really seriously. Someone taps the microphone in the hall again, so I dart back into the hall, looking up at the stage.

She's not there.

I glance at Mum. She shrugs. Zahra isn't there either.

Oh God.

Oh no.

Rushing back to Mr France, I wedge myself between him and Tiggy Spence's mum.

"Maya!" he protests.

"I'm really sorry," I say, in the vague direction of Tiggy's mum, "but my sister, Zahra – she's missing. She's gone, I think she's been kidnapped. Can you go out and get those policemen?"

# Chapter 7

If Zahra was here, she'd say I'd gone too far. But she isn't.

A perfectly dressed man called Inspector Khan is looking out of place seated on a small green plastic chair alongside DS Parker, who turns out to be a woman with strange taste in lipstick colour.

"Maya?" she says. "I see what you mean about the hair now."

"Her sister looks exactly the same," says Mr France. He is being my parent because my own parents and Granddad are talking to another lot of police who are sure that Zahra has run away with an imaginary boyfriend.

"So he thinks he's got you then?" says the inspector, speaking for the first time.

"Yes," I say. "But I didn't see the murder. I don't know why he would want me."

At that point Mum breaks free from the police who are questioning her and rushes over, brushing away Mr France and sitting right next to me, huge tears racing down her face.

"What are you doing sitting here?" she says to Inspector Khan. "My daughter's been kidnapped by a murderer!"

\* \* \*

The police drive us all home. And then we have a policewoman who makes us tea and tries to read stories to the twins.

I feel sick. Completely sick.

We could search. But there's no point in searching if she's been kidnapped.

There's a fluffy cardigan at the end of my bed. I pull it over my head to cut off the world, but the world's inside my head and it's accusing me of doing this.

"It's all my fault," I say out loud.

It isn't, I think. It's all the man's fault.

I don't make myself feel any better.

I sit on my bed looking at Zahra's duvet. There's a dent where she must have been sitting this morning to put on her shoes. Her pyjamas are in a heap on the floor so I pick them up and fold them neatly. I put her battered rabbit on the top and arrange his ears. They're soft. I pick him up and stroke him against my face.

Mum comes in. Her face is exploded and red, her eyes have practically disappeared. Dad's standing behind her. He looks grey and shocked. Mum kneels on the floor and starts to tidy under Zahra's bed. Dad stands in the doorway, listening to the conversation in the kitchen.

I can hear Granddad talking to the policewoman. "Any news?" I ask.

"No," says Mum, from under the bed. "But I'm sure they'll find her." Mum's voice trembles as she says it, and she wipes her tear-stained face on the corner of the duvet. Dad squeezes her shoulder. They look completely unlike my parents. They're like new exhausted people I've never seen before, old and young at the same time.

In the distance, another helicopter circles and a church bell strikes.

"Ten o'clock," says Dad.

"Oh, Maya," says Mum, and she lunges towards me, grabbing my arms, the tears bursting out again. "Maya – what are we going to do?"

* * *

Only the twins go to bed. The rest of us pace around the kitchen, waiting, listening to the policewoman talking on her lapel phone.

Inspector Khan arrives and asks me more questions.

"Will you get her back?" I ask.

The inspector pulls the crease of his trousers straight. He studies the skirting board as if it might hold the answer then nods his head.

"Don't worry," he says, not meeting my eye. "I'm sure we'll get your sister back."

I go back to our room and lie on Zahra's bed, clutching her rabbit and rocking and worrying. I stare into the mirror. A dark face, black hair, white streak, just like Zahra. Just like Dad.

Why couldn't they get it right?

Why didn't they take me?

41

# Chapter 8

At about half past four in the morning, Granddad cooks breakfast. The smell of toast floats into my nostrils and I wake up feeling almost normal until I remember that Zahra's gone.

Dustbin lorries grind through the streets and the traffic rumbles past the flat. The first helicopters of the day hover over the river and all life starts again.

It's Friday. I should be going to school. I should be really excited about the end-of-term party.

I stumble off the bed. I'm still wearing my school uniform.

Two new policemen are drinking coffee at the kitchen table.

"Morning Maya, love," says Granddad, extra cheerfully. "Your mum and dad are out in the van helping with the search. Fancy an egg?"

I notice the radio is burbling in the background, but Granddad reaches over and turns down the volume. I'm guessing Zahra's disappearance will be headline news.

"Anything?" I ask the policemen.

One of them shakes his head, the other doesn't even look at me.

Precious appears in the doorway, her heavy night-time nappy hanging below her knees and I force myself to smile. "Precious," I say. "Let's sort you out."

She runs to the bathroom ahead of me and lies on the floor, her legs in the air, expectant. I breathe through my mouth to undo the nappy and I'm just untangling her fingers from my hair when I hear a kerfuffle at the door.

Bare-bottomed, Precious springs to her feet to see what's going on and I follow.

Mum, Dad and a policeman burst into the flat closely followed by Zahra.

"Zahra!" I yell, racing down the passage to hug her.

"Maya!" she shouts, and I squeeze her as tight as I dare.

"What happened?" I say.

Precious races around our knees, dancing and shouting although she's no idea what's going on.

"We found her – outside the school!" says Dad.

"Well, I'd been there about a minute," says Zahra.

"Just a moment." Inspector Khan appears at the top of the stairs, behind Detective Sergeant Parker, whose lipstick has disappeared overnight. "We need to talk to Zahra before she forgets anything – if that's all right."

Zahra sits on a chair at the table, looking small. Everyone else stands in a circle around her, except for Inspector Khan. He takes off his overcoat. Underneath, he's wearing the same perfect suit. If he's slept in it, it doesn't show. He looks at a chair, carefully brushing the seat with his hand before sitting down. He takes a pair of tiny glasses from a case and balances them on his nose. His very dark eyes now seem larger. Detective Sergeant Parker stands behind, taking notes, while Inspector Khan watches Zahra very carefully. She's putting a brave face on it, but she's shaking, and I can see by the salt tracks on her cheeks that she's been crying.

"Tell us, in your own words—"

"So it all started when they stuck the bag over my head—"

"A bag? They put a bag over your head?" the inspector stops her.

"Yes – I went to the toilet, then back up the hallway, and I was actually on the back of the stage, behind the curtains. Someone came from behind, put something black over my head and then bundled me into a zippy holdall thingy. I could hear all the people in the hall, but they were so loud I don't suppose anyone could hear me shouting."

"It was very full, ever such a big crowd," says Mum, grabbing Dad's arm and smiling.

"Thank you," says Inspector Khan. "And then what?"

Granddad lands a plate of toast and marmalade in front of Zahra and she takes an enormous bite, thinking about her answer. "Then they blindfolded me."

"In the bag? Where?"

"After the bag, I think there was a car – then they unzipped the bag and tied something around my eyes and my wrists. In a room – all I saw for a titchy bit was some white ceiling."

"Paint? Plaster?" asks DS Parker.

Zahra shrugs. "Dunno – just white."

"Did you see any faces?" asks Mum.

The corner of the inspector's mouth twitches. "And did they ask anything?"

"They wanted my phone, so I handed it out to them. They asked if I'd shown the pictures to the police. I said I didn't have any pictures." She looks at me. "I said I wasn't you," she says, her lower lip trembling. "They wanted you."

There's a silence while the inspector looks from Zahra to me, and from me to Zahra. "How many people do you think there were?" he asks. "Take your time to answer."

Zahra chews her toast. I'm pretty sure she's already got the answer in her head, but she's probably trying to get it right. "One – maybe two, I'd say."

"Man – woman?" asks DS Parker, just before Mum does.

"I only ever heard a man. And he mostly wasn't speaking English."

"I know this is a long shot," says the inspector. "But do you think he might have been talking in say, French, with an English or Scottish accent?"

"I've no idea – he might have been," says Zahra.

The inspector sits back and stares at his manicured fingernails. "Did you get any impression of the size of your captor?"

Zahra runs her fingers around the top of a mug. "They picked me up really easily, as if I didn't weigh anything."

"A big man then?" says Mum.

"Yes," says Zahra, glancing at me. "A solid one."

* * *

I sit behind Zahra, my arms around her shoulders, while she snuggles into her duvet. The police are going to ask her more questions, but she's tired, I'm tired, so we've been let off for now. She flicks through her phone and updates her Facebook status to "free", and I shudder at the panic I felt when I knew she'd gone.

"Did you really not see them?" I ask.

She shrugs. "I really didn't."

"Was it scary?"

"Yes, it was terrifying." She folds her arms over Rabbit, protectively. "But I knew I wasn't very far away from home. The journey took hardly any time."

"Oh?"

"And at first I thought it was a sort of joke or something? You know, sixth-formers or Dad or someone. And then they started shouting at me – while I was still in the bag."

"Really?!"

"They were really cross when they realised I was me, and not you… At first they didn't believe me, but then I said we looked exactly the same…" She stops, and we look up at Mum and Inspector Khan who are standing in the doorway staring at us.

"What?" I ask. "What is it?"

"We've been talking," says Mum. "Me, the inspector and your dad. This man obviously wants you quite badly."

" Why?"

"Well, that's just one of the things we don't know," says the inspector. "It seems you saw something – something you shouldn't have. Without the camera card we don't know what, but you're a witness. And I don't think we can doubt he'd like to talk to you, not after what happened to your sister. So I think we have to make plans."

"Plans? Like what?"

# Chapter 9

I peel off my shirt and chuck it in the general direction of the dirty-clothes basket. Ishan comes over and hugs my legs, blows bubbles against my knees and lands a kiss on Zahra's rabbit. My fingers tremble as I undo the zip on my skirt.

Zahra sits on her bed and stares at the posters on our wall. "But why are you going so far?" she asks.

"To keep me safe," I say, trying to keep the wobble out of my voice.

"But they're going to leave a policeman here," she says.

"I know. But they don't think that's enough. I

suppose the shop's open all the time and—"

"But being sent to Auntie V's – I mean – that's harsh." Zahra shivers.

The last and only time we met Auntie V, one of her dogs bit me. For some reason she told *me* off rather than the dog and I cried all the way home. There was a boy there too. I didn't like him either. He stuck his tongue out at me and poured salt over my ice cream but I didn't say anything because I didn't want to get into trouble with her again. It wasn't much fun.

Auntie V's house was cold and gloomy, and in the middle of mud. Miles and miles of mud.

I shake my head. That can't be true. No one could live in the middle of miles and miles of mud.

"It'll be fine," I say in the end, stuffing all my most boring clothes into Dad's wheely suitcase and then at the last minute adding my new parka, just in case it isn't all mud.

"It won't be fine for me, I'll miss you," says Zahra, picking my iPod off the floor and dropping it into the zippy bit of the bag. "How will you manage without me?"

"I don't know," I say, hugging her tight and sniffing back a tear.

"And you won't be here for the end of term," she says. "You won't be able to go to the party."

"Yup," I say, sniffing back another tear. "True."

She winds the cables around my chargers and hands them to me. "But why Auntie V?" she asks again.

"Because it's as far away and as safe as she can be," says Mum, rustling in the doorway. She's wearing a huge black waterproof and wellies, and looks as if she's about to go fishing off the Scottish coast, in a gale, with her bare hands. "Ready, Maya?"

"Mama," says Ishan, sitting on her wellington. "Mama."

Mum bends down and picks him up, flinging him under her arm. "Keep out the way, trouble," she says, stamping off along the landing. "Dennis!" she shouts. "Can you keep an eye on the twins – properly."

There's a grunt from Granddad in the kitchen.

"Take Rabbit," says Zahra, holding the rabbit out to me.

"But don't you need him?" I say, taking him in my hands and bending his ears down over his eyes.

"Yes – but I've got Mum and Dad and home, you need him more."

"If you're sure," and I kiss her on the top of the head.

She holds my hand. "Watch your back, sis," she says in a mock-American accent.

Smiling, but not trusting myself to speak, I jam Rabbit in my tote bag and drag the wheely suitcase along the corridor, stopping behind Granddad who's sitting at the table.

Granddad looks up. "Your Auntie V's, eh? You gonna be all right, Maya? Out there in the countryside?"

I nod. "Yeah. It'll be OK," I say. Or at least my mouth says it, even though my heart doesn't.

"You're not worried, are you?" he says.

"No," I lie, my stomach doing a flip. He's so old, so frail. I can't tell him that I'm worried about everything. The things I know and the things I don't.

"I'll miss you, girl. Won't be the same without my little mechanic by my side." He picks up an oily piece of metal that I recognise as a crankshaft. "I was hoping to get this put together before Christmas."

"The police'll get it sorted out soon, I'm sure," I say. "I'll be back before you know it."

"That's my girl," he says, meaninglessly. "Take care of yourself. Say hello to your auntie. Tell her she's always welcome here."

"Right," says Mum, barrelling past. "Ready? The police said we need to leave as soon as possible – in case – well, just as soon as possible."

# Chapter 10

Mum's not a good driver. She's especially bad in traffic and she makes these anxious noises as we fight our way out of London in the van.

I sit in the middle of the front seat gazing out at all the cars jammed across the road. We're barely moving. We've barely moved for an hour.

"Mum," I say. "Do you think that man would try to find me in Wales?".

Mum goes silent for a long time. She chews her lip and grips the wheel, staring into the traffic. "As your granddad would say – better safe than sorry."

"But he could come to the shop – he could find

you, or the twins – he could have hung on to Zahra to get to me. Do keep her safe, Mum – don't let her go to friends' houses on her own."

"Don't worry, I won't, and if he comes to the shop – plenty of hammers to bop him on the head." She stops and goes quiet for a while. "But seriously, they're sticking an undercover policeman in the shop. I don't think we're in danger."

"Do you think I'll be safe halfway up a mountain?"

Mum doesn't answer that, just reaches over and squeezes my hand.

She doesn't smile. She doesn't do a reassuring laugh. Nothing.

Small dots of rain appear on the windscreen and Mum switches on the wipers.

We move a little further out of London. The cars flow past on all sides.

"Do you think we're being followed?" I ask, looking out into the wing mirror.

"No," says Mum, unconvincingly.

The van has "Southwark Sanitary Solutions" written all over the side. We wouldn't be that difficult to find. But apart from a fourteen-year-old Nissan Micra that failed its MOT last week, we don't have anything else to travel in. I watch a blue estate behind us until it peels off and disappears.

We inch forwards. Blue lights flash in the mirror and a police car threads its way through the traffic, pulling alongside and then bouncing on to the hard shoulder.

"Is that for us?" I ask.

"I wish," says Mum.

And we go back to silent anxiety.

\* \* \*

I must fall asleep at some point, because the next time I'm aware of our surroundings we're on an almost completely dark motorway, the engine humming noisily, being overtaken periodically by cars thundering on into the night. The windscreen wipers are still going but the rain's much heavier now. Splotty.

It might almost be sleet.

"Where are we?"

"Somewhere near the Severn Bridge," says Mum.

We thunder on down the road.

"What's Auntie V like?" I ask.

"Oh, she's OK really," says Mum. "Very bossy older sister."

We pass a load of lights.

"Is he called Ollie? Her son."

"Yes. Ollie. I don't know him very well. He's about fourteen — and all I know is he's a really talented horse rider. Oops — sorry." Mum weaves on to the white line. I hope she's not too tired to do this. "I wonder if there's a service station anywhere soon?"

"We passed one just now, I think," I say.

"Actually — I'm fine. Check the glovebox, love, see if Dad's left anything in there?"

Opening the glovebox releases a cascade of old wrappers, paper cups and delivery notes. There's no light, so I have to put my hand inside and feel for anything solid. At the back, near the bottom, I find a bag that appears to be unopened.

"Liquorice?" I say, using the glow of the dashboard lights to read the packet. "I quite like liquorice."

"Ha," says Mum. "Typical. I hate the stuff. Your dad hates liquorice too, he must have bought it by accident."

Ruffling the remaining wrappers, I manage to scoop up four things that might be toffees. "Chocolate eclair?" I offer.

"How old?" asks Mum.

I squeeze it experimentally. "It's soft," I say.

"I'll pass on that," she says, shifting in her seat.

I check my phone. No messages.

I stare into the wing mirror. There's a lone set of headlights behind. "Could that car be following us?" I ask.

"Na," says Mum. "You've watched too many films. Go back to sleep."

I type, *lonely*, into the phone, and then delete it.

As I'm staring at the screen, a message comes in from Zahra.

*Missing you already. Come home soon. xxx*

# Chapter 11

It's nearly eight o'clock when the headlights of the van catch the sign on the side of the road. "Valley Trekking Centre. Closed."

"At last," says Mum, grinding the gears and wrenching the van on to a narrow-walled track. The sleet is still falling, but thickly now, and a pack of ice has formed on either side of the windscreen.

We lurch along the track, thumping into potholes. The engine revs wildly, and Mum clings to the steering wheel.

"Blimey," she says, as a white bird looms out of the snow and vanishes above us into the blizzard.

Jolted awake I peer along the track. The traffic jams of London feel a lifetime away. The track tips and instead of climbing, we start to slide down the ruts, Mum leaning on the brake pedal, the walls closing in on either side until we reach a tall pair of gates that lead into an enclosed yard.

"Blimey," says Mum again.

I was right about the mud. They do live in the middle of a mud patch. A *huge* mud patch. The headlights of the van highlight the crests of the mud and Mum slithers to a halt near the small semi-circle of light that marks the front door.

"Hmm," says Mum. "Seems more remote in the winter."

For a minute, we sit in the van and watch the sleet streaking through the headlights, settling on the tufts of grass sticking out around the front door. Between us and the tufts of grass is more mud. That and some grit, and slushy snow.

* * *

I fall out of the van door. It's high and the mud catches me by surprise and squishes straight over the top of my Converse into my socks.

"Come on, Maya," says Mum. "You'll freeze."

Grabbing the bag of liquorice, I jam it in my

pocket. If no one else likes it, then I might as well take it.

We stand in the icy squish, waiting for the front door to open.

"Sarah!" Auntie V throws open the front door and three tall stinky dogs press their way around her, sniffing at us and thwacking their tails against the door frame. I wonder which one bit me last time?

Auntie V pushes them away and drags us in from the snow. "Bloody freezing," she says, ushering us down a stone-floored hallway to a huge heavy door, hanging with mangy rugs. "Come in here, Ollie's got the fire going really well tonight. Come on, come on." She herds us and the dogs and shuts the door.

We enter a fug. Woodsmoke, soup, wet dogs. Warm, but definitely damp.

Perching on a collapsed sofa, my backpack guarding my feet, I grab a cushion to keep my bum from the broken spring sticking up through the base. It's a kitchen, a dining room and a sort of living room, all in one. By the sofa is a huge fireplace with a wood burner. Over by a heavily curtained window is a long table with a bench, and a laptop.

Behind the laptop is a boy. Ollie?

"Say hello." His mum taps his shoulder.

"Do I have to?" he says, without looking up.

Auntie V nudges him but says nothing.

I gaze very intently at the small square of orange in the front of the wood burner.

I do not want to be here.

Mum must sense it because she squeezes my hand, and then springs into life, going all gushy and chatty and Auntie V starts ladling something from a black pan simmering on a huge stove thing into unmatched bowls.

"The traffic was awful leaving London, and then the rain started – so it's been a bit of a marathon." They're both talking too loud.

"Ah," says Auntie V, studying something in the ladle and tipping it down the sink. "But you found us OK?"

"Oh yes," says Mum. "But I'm glad the snow didn't get going too much."

"So why didn't the police bring her here?" asks Auntie V.

"I think the inspector felt it was better if she came – incognito. They're going to station a policeman here though, if that's all right with you?"

In front of us, the wood burner spits and hums. I'm aware of my mum's accent. London, casual. Auntie V sounds different. Welsh?

"Fine — whatever it takes," says Auntie V.

She sloshes stuff into the bowls and drops the ladle in the sink. "We're due very heavy snow later on tomorrow, so you'd better get going sharpish in the morning, you don't want to get stuck."

"Course," says Mum. She glances at me, and then at Ollie.

"Do you think they'll get on?" she whispers to Auntie V.

"Course," Auntie V replies. "Bound to. In the end."

I glance up at Ollie and catch him staring at me with obvious disgust on his face.

Mum smiles vaguely in my direction and checks her phone. "No signal," she says to the room and stands by her sister. "Anything I can do?"

Auntie V points at a set of drawers. "Get four spoons out."

\* \* \*

After the soup I go to bed in an icy and slightly smelly room at the front of the house overlooking the yard. Auntie V gives me a hot-water bottle and a glass of water and drives the dogs away down the stairs but not before they've slobbered all over my bedcovers.

Maybe it's the dogs I can smell.

"Sorry," says Auntie V. "They normally sleep in here when it's cold."

Mum comes in with me and sits on my bed. She looks really tired, and for a moment she sags forward to rub her eyes before sitting up brightly and pulling a reassuring smile over her face. She ruffles the long white streak in my hair and runs a finger over my cheek.

"What?" I ask, swinging my feet up on to the freezing mattress and jamming them into the arctic wastes under the eiderdown.

"Thought I'd kiss you goodnight," says Mum. "So," she prods a faded bowl of potpourri, releasing a cloud of dust. "I bet you'll have a lovely time up here."

"Do you really think so?" I say. "It's kind of – ancient. And Ollie obviously hates me."

"Don't be silly – he's an only child, I expect he's just not used to having someone in his space."

"Hmm," I say, thinking of the expression on his

face.

"And it's the countryside, Maya, people do things differently here. The pace of life is slower. You'll have to adjust to them." Mum sounds like she's reciting something she learned from a book.

She brushes imaginary crumbs from the eiderdown.

"Have you told Auntie V that I'm a vegetarian?" I ask.

"Of course," says Mum. "She knows."

"When will the policeman come? The one that's on duty with us?" I ask.

Mum glances at her phone, which is as blank as mine. "I don't know, love – soon I imagine."

"When will you come back?" I ask.

"Oh," Mum looks vague. "Not so very long, I don't expect. The police will get their man and we'll pop back and get you. A few days. Until then, keep out from under V's feet, be good and helpful."

She pulls the eiderdown straight. "I think the police are right. You're safer here. Miles from anywhere – no one could possibly run into you. At home we'd have had to imprison you in the flat. And that wouldn't have been any fun."

"No," I say, wondering just how much fun I can

have here in this damp dusty farmhouse.

"Anyway — I'm pooped." She says, pulling my head forward and kissing my hair. She stands and goes all busy tucking me into bed and folding up jeans, before turning off the main light. "I imagine you are too."

"Sarah!" Auntie V calls from along the landing.

"Night sweetie," says Mum from the doorway. "Might have to go early in the morning, take care."

"Can't you stay tomorrow?"

Mum shakes her head. "I can't leave Dad and Granddad for long. The twins are too much, and we're so busy just now, just before Christmas. You'll be fine without me." She pauses for a moment.

"Sarah! Do you want to know where you're sleeping?" yells Auntie V.

"Sleep well, be careful," says Mum, closing the door.

"Bye — night," I call and listen to her footsteps on the floorboards until they disappear.

* * *

I worm my way into the bottom of the bed, crushed by the heavy old eiderdown. It's so cold inside that, despite the hot-water bottle and the furry thermal sheet, my feet freeze instantly. I lie in the dark listening to the wind and the sleet against the windows.

I so want home. I rub my feet together, trying to get some heat, longing for Zahra's comfort. If she were here I could coil into her for warmth and safety. I need her now more than I've ever needed her. She'll be on her own in bed, but she won't, because everyone else is there. They're together all in the flat, hugger-mugger, Granddad would say. All cosy. And me, out here, alone.

"Mum?" I say out loud, but I can hear her downstairs, talking to Auntie V, and I suppose they're sisters too. They need their own time.

I climb out of bed, rummage in my suitcase for Zahra's rabbit, fail to find it, and climb back into bed slightly more miserable. I must have left it in the van. I'll ask Mum first thing.

# Chapter 12

Sometime in the darkest hours, I begin to doze, needing a wee but not needing it so much I want to run down the freezing landing to the toilet. Headlights track across the ceiling and something does a million-point-turn in the drive.

"Mum!" I register, slightly too late, and see the van vanish between the gateposts and off into the sleet. "Mum."

As the van disappears, a figure comes out of the house. Auntie V? She's swaddled in coats and hats and picks her way through the mud to the other side of the yard. She slips two bolts on a vast door and pulls it open. Inside, I glimpse a large shed glowing with yellow light reflected on hay and straw. Steam rises from the ground and she closes the door again. A lone dog trots into view, sniffs the air and comes back towards the house.

I once saw a book in the library called *Cold Comfort Farm*. This is it. *Cold Comfort Farm*.

I check my tablet. 07.12. No Wi-Fi signal. No anything signal.

Not knowing what to do I climb back into bed and hug my knees and wish really hard that I hadn't seen anything from that bus. If I could turn back time, I'd have looked the other way, then I'd be at home for the end-of-term party, which is tonight. I would have worn my green dress, and Zahra's platforms. Or maybe jeans. I'd have coloured my white streak purple – just for the party. I try to imagine what everyone else will be wearing, and for a second I kid myself that I could catch a train up to London and just go to the party and come back.

My stomach rumbles.

I could go downstairs – but then, Auntie V's out with the horses, which would leave me alone with Ollie.

As it gets light outside I look around the room.

It's all wrong, all the furniture's in the wrong place. I'd like to move it around, but for starters I rearrange the wooden elephants on the mantelpiece so that they're talking to each other. Somehow that's better.

Dusting the window sill with my elbow I look down into the yard. There's no policeman yet, but I must be safe. This place is like a castle. Walls as thick as a bunker's. Only one way in, high windows. And outside, miles and miles of nothing. There's nowhere to hide. I can see why Mum thought it would be good. It really is remote.

In the distance something moves against one of the walls.

Probably a sheep.

Sleet turns to snow and snow back to sleet and then it stops. My breath fogs the glass.

I'm feeling feary again, which is silly. It's perfectly safe here.

Right now – the shop will be heaving with people picking up last-minute orders for Christmas. Mirrors for over the basin, rubber washers to mend the kitchen tap before the relations arrive, whole bathroom suites to be fitted overnight. Granddad'll be running on caffeine, keeping it going like a ballet, Dad'll be out delivering like crazy, and if she's home, Mum'll be on the phone listening to some really tedious story about three-way valves from a plumber in Lambeth.

With a sock I clean the condensation off my bedroom window. I'm staring up at the hill to where I saw the sheep, when a white police Land Rover edges slowly into the mud in front of the house, and two policemen get out.

They come to the door and knock and I hear voices below. One of the policemen gets back into the car and it slithers backwards up the track. The remaining policeman's voice is clear and loud. Auntie V is quieter, but I gather that he gets offered a cup of tea and accepts.

This, I realise, is the most exciting thing that's going to happen today.

I get dressed and use some facial wipes to get yesterday's mud off my shoes. It's not very effective, and they're never going to look as good as they did, but I carry them downstairs to dry next to the stove thing.

There's no one there so I investigate the kitchen cupboards. I discover that Auntie V has some really old cornflakes, and that the milk comes in bottles. I look at the bread – lumpy, brown and seedy – and decide I'll pass on it. Instead, I boil myself an egg, which I eat standing up in the kitchen with the dogs snurfling around my elbows.

"How am I supposed to eat anything with you lot interfering all the time?" I say out loud, holding my spoon above my head with one hand and protecting my egg with the other.

"You can't," says a voice from the doorway.

Ollie.

"Hi," I say. "I just wondered—"

"I don't care," he says, opening a cupboard and pulling out a bag of porridge oats. "Da de da de da – don't tell me, I'm not very interested."

He pours oats into a saucepan and sloshes milk over the top. Crashing the pan on to the stove top he chucks a spoon at the pan, missing, and sends it skittering over the side. The dogs leap to grab it and rush off fighting over it while Ollie swears under his breath. I stare. Appalled. No one, not even Tiggy Spence, has ever been that rude.

I open my mouth to say something but the front door opens and Auntie V comes in.

"Ah, Maya," she says, dropping something that might be a saddle on the back of the sofa. "Great to see you together. Ollie's bored up here, it'll be good to have someone his own age for a while. I expect you two are going to get on like a house on fire."

\* \* \*

A house on fire is just about right.

"Could I go riding?" I ask later on, surprising myself.

"I don't think that's a good idea, Maya. Do you?" Auntie V looks up from an ancient looking recipe book and raises her eyebrows. "But I'll ask our police guard, Sergeant Lewis."

She goes out into the yard and Ollie throws himself on the floor and rolls around hooting with exaggerated laughter.

"What's so funny?" I say.

"You – on a horse." He pushes himself across the floor on his back. "Like you even *can* ride."

"How d'you know I can't?"

Auntie V swings back through the door. "The sergeant's not sure. Why not have a bath, instead? It'll make the day feel better. Up the stairs on the left."

*A bath?*

I leave the room and traipse up the stairs thinking dark thoughts about Ollie and wondering if a bath is really going to make today any better. I poke my nose into the bathroom. It's damp with black mould growing in the corners and it's cold. Very, very cold.

I peer into the tub. "Ooohh!"

There's a huge black spider sitting in the middle of the yellow-stained enamel. I can deal with most things, but not spiders.

"What is it?!" Auntie V comes running up the stairs.

"Spider," I say, pointing.

Auntie V laughs. "Ollie," she says. "Help your cousin with this spider, would you?"

"Why?"

"Because my hands are covered in flour and perhaps she doesn't like them," says Auntie V.

"Doesn't like spiders," echoes Ollie in a baby voice as he climbs the stairs. "Auntie V, I'm scared of Incy Wincy and I want you to take him away and make the bathroom all pink and fluffy cos I'm a princess and I come from princess land."

"Ollie!" Auntie V snaps.

I retreat to my bedroom, listening to the clanking as Ollie presumably chases the spider out.

"Done," he shouts. "Your Ladyship," he adds,

just loud enough for me to hear.

"Thank you," I say coming out on to the landing.

"My pleasure," he says, throwing something black at my hair which turns out to be a sock, but makes me jump all the same.

# Chapter 13

I have a bath where the water goes cold in seconds, and as I emerge covered in goose pimples I hear hooves in the yard. *They've* gone riding.

So I rearrange the bedroom – I don't care that it's not my house. If I'm going to be stuck here with idiots like Ollie, I need to have a sanctuary. Dragging the bed, I stick it under the window and push the skanky chest of drawers to where I can't see it on the other side of the door.

I pull the bedspread so that it's half folded over at the foot and empty the bowl of potpourri out of the window. I chuck some dirty socks (not mine) out on the landing and get all my make-up and creams out and arrange them on the window sill. Finally, I take a purple-and-pink scarf that I bought in Camden Market, and drape it over the bed head, so that the bedside light casts warm shadows on the cold white walls.

"Yes," I say to the room, sitting on the bed so that I can look out of the window and keep my feet warm under the bedspread. I lean back against the pillows and stare at the view. I expect there are people who would say it's fabulous. Even people who'd pay to stay here.

Not me, though.

I have another thought and jam everything from the top drawer of the chest into the other three drawers. Although I could unpack my bag, I've got a better plan and I fill the top drawer with all the ugly things in the room (of which there are loads) and display the nicer things. The curtains are a horrible flower pattern, so I turn them round and get the cream lining instead.

I hang my school backpack on the back of the door. It's a cool Korean bird design. Like a picture.

Much better.

Checking my phone I see there's a faint Wi-Fi

signal, but even after searching the house I can't find the router anywhere to log in, so I give up and search for fairylights instead.

Downstairs, the phone rings. I watch it vibrating.

"Do you think I should answer that?" I ask Sergeant Lewis.

He shakes his head. "Better not. Let it ring for now."

"So you don't think I'm safe here?" I say.

"No – I wouldn't say that. You're perfectly safe," says the sergeant. "My colleague is out there checking the lanes, no one can get within ten miles. I'm just a bit of garnish so to speak."

The garnish goes back to lean against the front door and I listen to the phone until it goes silent.

\* \* \*

"Have you got broadband?" I ask when Auntie V and Ollie return.

"D'you mean, like London-super-fibre-princess-standard broadband? In which case – no."

"Ollie!" Auntie V snaps and turns to me, a tight smile on her face. "Yes – we do, the password's on the back of the router thingy, which is in my bedroom, under the bed. Ollie must know it by heart." She glances across at him, but Ollie grins,

78

shaking his head.

"Soreee," he says. "Simply can't remember. Anyway, it comes from Feeble dot com — and doesn't work properly."

"He's right, it is a bit hit-and-miss — can take ages to load. The telephone exchange is about 15 miles away. But it's there if you want to try it. "

"It'll never support three people using it at once," mutters Ollie. "If *she* uses it, then I won't be able to Skype Gethin!"

"Oh dear," I say. Not meaning it at all.

I go up to do battle with the dust bunnies under Auntie V's bed, where I find a tiny router, with a tiny code.

*Sweetocean 121*

Of course he knows it by heart. He just wanted me to get covered in dust.

The phone rings again.

I hear Auntie V pick it up. I listen, hoping for Mum.

"Hello?" she says. "Valley Trekking Centre."

There's a pause, then: "Hello," says Auntie V. "Anyone there?"

A spoon clangs on a bowl.

"That's odd," she says in the end. "Nothing."

* * *

I try the Wi-Fi from my bedroom.

I try Google.

It can't load and I get a picture of a dinosaur.

After at least ten minutes it finally loads my e-mails and I write one to Zahra. *Queuing* it says.

For ages.

And then it just gives up.

I suspect that Ollie is using every scrap of Wi-Fi.

On purpose.

I think about filling his bed with biscuit crumbs and then think about mobile-phone signals. I wonder if you can get one on the mountain?

* * *

"Auntie V, can we go up the mountain — for a walk? — I need some fresh air. Please."

"I'll ask Sergeant Lewis," she says. "I suppose the sheep could do with hay. I was going to send Ollie, but…"

Sergeant Lewis and his friend in the four-by-four say we can. They're ninety-nine per cent sure that no one's out there. Only ninety-nine per cent, mind.

"Haven't you got anything more sensible?" she asks, looking at my low-heeled boots.

80

I shake my head.

Ollie lets out a long and exaggerated sigh before sitting down at the laptop. "Expect she only wears glass slippers."

"I do that on Tuesdays," I say, "not Saturdays."

"These'll do," says Auntie V, holding down a giggle and handing me a pair of black crusty wellingtons that almost fit.

It's the first time I've been out of the house since I arrived, and in the fading daylight, I see that it's actually a U-shaped yard. The farmhouse, the stables and another barn full of hay make up the two long sides, and a walled garden at the bottom is the short bit. There are no windows on the outer side of any of it, so it's all closed in with only the narrow gateway as an opening.

"It's really well protected," I say to Auntie V. "Like a fortress."

"It is – it was built six hundred years ago to withstand marauders and snow. In theory no one can get in without going through the gateway."

We load up a wheelbarrow and swing out of the yard and up a track that leads straight towards the mountain.

End of the day winter sunlight falls yellow on

the short grass in front of us, and we stumble up between high walls. Two small railway lines run all the way up the hill embedded in the earth.

"What are these?" I ask.

"They're for the trucks," says Auntie V, with no more explanation.

"Oh," I say, kicking at the rusty track half in half out of the ground.

All I can hear are birds. No helicopters, no cars. The silence is almost too big for me and I can't help feeling as though I'm being watched. Perhaps this wasn't such a good idea.

A huge bird circles overhead. Maybe it's the watcher.

We walk on up the track, the dogs racing around our legs, breaking up the awkward silence.

One of the dogs wanders back and lopes alongside me. It's almost friendly.

"She likes you," says Auntie V.

"Does she?" I ask. "What's her name?"

"Megan, she's the fastest of the three." She ruffles the brown hair around the dog's neck. "Aren't you? So what's your sister like?" she asks, opening a field gate.

"She's all ice skating and nail varnish," I say.

"We're quite different but we get on."

"It must have been awful when she was kidnapped," says Auntie V.

"It was," I say.

"And what about you — what are you like — what do you like to do?"

"Seeing my friends, and fixing things."

"Like what?" asks Auntie V.

"Oh, mechanical things, things with engines," I say.

Auntie V laughs. "Really?"

"Well Granddad does, so I do it with him — I like making old things come back to life."

"Of course — I'd forgotten he did that — Ollie loves fixing things too. He's got this ancient bulldozer — it's tiny — not like one of those huge things you get on the motorways — it's actually got a trailer too. He loves fiddling about with it."

We push on up the hill. It's starting to get dark. "He's spent all year fixing it. All summer. He's been very determined about it. But then, Ollie's very determined about everything. Stubborn."

"Where is it — I haven't seen it at the farm?"

"Oh, it's up the mountain in the mine — between you and me, I don't think it's working properly, I don't like to ask," she laughs. "He can be difficult."

"Certainly can," I say under my breath.

"His father's a bit of a disappointment to him and he gets a little lonely stuck up here."

"Oh," I say, trying to feel sympathetic, and failing. "So you don't know what's wrong with it?"

"It won't start, although I think he's fixed everything that needs fixing and he's spent hours on the Internet trying to work out why it won't work."

In my pocket, my phone buzzes and buzzes.

"You've got a signal!" says Auntie V, reaching into her pocket.

We both pause and read our mobiles, their yellow light now seeming quite bright in the winter twilight.

*How are you? Missing you!* ☺ From Zahra.

*Missing you too, but am OK,* I say. *Any news? And Pls can you ask Granddad how to start an old bulldozer? Everything fixed. Won't start. E-mail me too.*

*What?*

*Just ask him XXX.*

I see if I can get Google to load, but my screen freezes and I give up.

When we reach them I see that the sheep are

horned balls of brown with extra grubby bits around their bums. They bleat together as we approach and cluster around the gate nuzzling at our armfuls of hay. They don't seem worried by the dogs.

"They're Soays – lovely animals, and pretty rare. They're very tough though. Mountain sheep."

"Oh," I say. "They look like goats to me."

"They do, don't they – but I can assure you they're sheep. Now shake the hay out and scatter it along the wall, otherwise only the bullies will get it."

The sheep stumble over each other in search of food, grabbing strandy mouthfuls from flattened piles, shoving and pushing and even grabbing hay from each other's mouths. They're kind of cute.

"They've nearly eaten it all," I say. "Don't they eat the grass?"

"They do," says Auntie V, "but there isn't enough at this time of year, so we give them hay every day. They're a terrible nuisance, but they're good to run with horses, and there are so few of them, I feel duty-bound to hang on to the herd – and the lamb's delicious."

"Oh," I say. "I don't eat meat."

"Oh yes, I'd forgotten. Remind me to make something else for you this evening."

My phone buzzes again. I glance down.

*Granddad says bang the fuel pump with a hammer?!?!!*

"Don't worry, I'm fine with vegetables," I say, absently thinking about hammers and bulldozers.

"It's not a problem, it'll be fine," says Auntie V, picking up the last section of hay and flinging it across the field. "I'll put my mind to it."

# Chapter 14

But she doesn't because supper is four plates with lasagne heaped on them. Meaty lasagne. We sit in almost silence and I pick at my plate. I can eat the cheese and I try to scrape the top layer of pasta from the beef below. It tastes of meat but I swallow it. I'm starving.

Sergeant Lewis wolfs his down, and rattles on about nothing. He's probably been unnerved by the silence, especially Ollie's, but even though he's got a beautiful Welsh accent, the long string of incoherent valley gossip starts to get pretty boring.

Auntie V asks polite questions. "So how long

ago did your daughter graduate?"

I pick some carrot pieces out of the goo. This is a very long way from the food they'll be having at the party. I wonder if I could pass the meat across to the dogs? One of them, Megan I think, is lying in front of the wood burner, one eye on the table. I take a forkful and lower it towards the flagstone floor. She bounds forward and snaffles it straightaway.

"Now, that'll be summer 2013 – or was it 14? Let me think…"

Ollie's watching me with this really irritating smirk on his face.

"What you staring at?" I say to him across the table. If I keep the meat on the left of my plate it's just about possible to disentangle the edible cheese.

Megan begs at my side.

"Picky," says Ollie, raising an eyebrow. "Why don't you just eat it?"

"Do you not like it, Maya?" asks Auntie V and then she claps her hand to her mouth and grabs my plate. "God – I'm so sorry, I completely forgot – I'll do you some noodles, or pasta. So sorry, love."

Ollie leans back, and lets out another of those dramatic sighs. "Do you mean she doesn't eat meat?" he asks no one in particular. "Do you even eat fish?"

"No I don't as a matter of fact. I have principles about eating living things."

"Seriously?" he says. "So not only do I have to give up my bedroom but we have to eat nuts just because the princess won't eat coochie-coo baby animals."

"Ollie – don't be so rude," snaps Auntie V, rushing from the table and slamming a wet pan on the stove so that it hisses and judders. Megan gives up on the meat and slopes back to the fire.

I wonder whether to mention the bulldozer and Granddad's fix. But then I decide Ollie's being so mean I'll keep it to myself. So we sit in silence for a while before I suddenly find myself saying, "Your bedroom? That'll be why it smells so bad."

"Ha!" says Sergeant Lewis.

"What?" says Ollie.

"Boys' changing rooms. Definitely boys' changing rooms." I pinch my nose.

He opens his mouth to protest and I can see him planning his next move. "Going to smell worse now though because you've been in there. It's going to smell of your stupid fake flowery muck. Stuff out of bottles and sprays, all made up in some poncy laboratory – because *you're worth it.*"

"Better than underpants," I say, leaning back and staring him out. "Anyway – I've rearranged it." I stick the biggest smile I can across my face. "So it's nicer in there now."

"Really?" says Sergeant Lewis, looking across at Ollie who goes dark and furious.

"Here you are, Maya, dear," says Auntie V, slapping down a plate of brown pasta with a tomato and some grated cheese.

"Thank you," I say, cheerily, launching into the food and pretending to look really happy about it. Ollie's black mood creeps across the table. But I can pretend it's not happening.

It's a little like eating gravel, extra chewy and gritty, and I don't want to think about the stinky cheese too much so I just keep on shovelling it in.

Sergeant Lewis chuckles his thanks and goes to put the kettle on.

The phone rings and Auntie V grabs it.

"Hello?" she says. "Hello?" She shakes the receiver. "I can't hear you," she says and after a moment, puts it back down.

"How many times now?" asks the sergeant.

"Three," she says, looking at the phone. "Anyway, I should have remembered. Your dad's a vegetarian of course. But your mum isn't — or at least she wasn't when we were kids."

"No — she and Granddad still eat sausages."

During our conversation, Ollie has been doing a series of massive yawns, slumping further and further into his seat and patting his mouth with his hand.

"So you grew up in our house?" I'm going to keep talking, just to annoy him.

She nods again.

"Yup," says Auntie V. "I grew up looking at the underneath of the railway bridge, over the plumbing-supply shop, listening to the bells of Southwark Cathedral with my dad fixing old motorbikes in the kitchen, sticking the crankcases in the oven and smoking out the road."

From the corner of my eye I see Ollie raise his head to stare at his mum, but I don't turn my head to look at him.

"He still does that," I say. "He still loves fixing things and I help."

"And what do you do?" says Ollie. "Wipe the oil from pieces of metal with a cotton bud? Make flowery covers for bike helmets?"

"No," I say. "I grind the valves and cook the crankcases, actually. I've taken apart carburettors and put them back together again. I've cleaned the spark plugs, rewired the wiring. Made a cog. You name it, I've done it," I say, flushing a little. It's *almost* completely true.

"I bet. It used to drive your gran mad, although she was just as bad, taking lawnmowers apart on that balcony, dropping the screws over the edge into the street below. It's genetic," she says to Ollie.

"What was that?" Sergeant Lewis peers out the kitchen window.

"What?" Auntie V looks suddenly anxious.

"Something glinted, up the track. I'll go out and check," he says.

"Is that a good idea?" Auntie V joins him at the window. "Shouldn't you stay here? Or I could go out with you?"

"Mum?" says Ollie, looking anxious.

"Don't," I say.

"I don't expect it's anything — just a spot of moonlight on a tin can — I'll make a phone call," says Sergeant Lewis. "Just in case."

# Chapter 15

"Well, they're coming anyway," says the sergeant, putting down the phone. "And we're to stay indoors."

I pick up my tablet and try to feel normal, but my heart's going poundy and I can sense that we're all feeling nervous. Clicking on Facebook, I try to get it to load. But the maddening little circle just goes round and round. It's ten to nine. Everyone else will be at the school party. There'll be brilliant food from Borough Market. Everyone always does brilliant food, lots of baba ganoush, and hummus, and those little chilli peppers stuffed with cheese.

And someone will have brought music, and the school hall will be all lit up with fairy lights and people will be dancing and being really funny, and singing along, and it'll be great and embarrassing. And they'll all be wearing party gear. Melita will have her new boots, and Keri will have something really expensive and original, and they'll mostly be wearing loads of make-up and false eyelashes and... I stare at the grubby rug on the floor. Dog-chewed and dog-walked-on.

"What's that you're looking at?" asks Ollie.

"Just trying to load Facebook," I say. "There's a party tonight."

"Oh," he says. But he doesn't say anything horrible.

*Rat – Tat – Tat*

We all jump, and the sergeant goes to the front door.

"She's in here," he says. An icy blast comes in with the visitors and I catch a glimpse of hard moonlit frost outside.

"Thank you." It's Inspector Khan, this time with a policewoman I haven't seen before and a nervous-looking woman with a sketchbook. Inspector Khan's incredibly clean suit looks really out of place here.

"Can I offer you tea? Coffee? Soup?" says Auntie V. "Or I've got a bit of lasagne left over? How are you, Helen?"

"Coffee'll do us, thanks V," says the policewoman. "I've got a pie in the oven for tea – Inspector Khan'll stay the night with us on the put-up bed." She places her bum on the back of an exploding old armchair and kicks off her boots. She's obviously used to the house. "I'll put him back on the train in the morning."

The inspector doesn't look thrilled about the night on the put-up bed but flashes a quick insincere smile at Helen. He looks around the room, taking it in, and brushes the seat of the sofa as he sits down. I know from experience it won't make any difference, he's going to get up covered in dog hair. He takes out a neat notebook and an expensive-looking pen and places the same pair of neat specs that he wore yesterday on his nose.

The nervous woman perches on a piece of furniture that I know is supposed to be a coffee table.

"Right," says Inspector Khan. "Right. Maya."

"Sergeant Lewis saw something on the track.

Should we be scared?" I ask.

The inspector moves his head about in an I-agree-with-you-but-I-don't-want-you-to-be-scared way, which tells me I should be scared.

"Maya." He interlocks his fingers, flips his hands over and clicks his elbows straight, raising them over his head, stretching. He looks as if he's going to be here for a while and once again, all the stuff that happened in London seems real. I *did* see a body. I *did* see a man with a gun. He *did* see me.

"Are you looking for him?" I ask.

"Of course," the inspector says. "Of course. But I want to ask you some questions and I want you to tell me about the woman. Lianne here has come up from Cardiff – she's very good at likenesses."

Lianne who is very good at likenesses tries an unconfident smile before tipping coffee over her sketchbook and ineffectually mopping it up with a scrap of tissue.

"So can we start with what anyone was wearing – any distinguishing features?" she says.

I sit back against the cushions and stare at the ceiling, trying really hard to remember anything. Anything at all.

* * *

It takes a while. We eat half a packet of bourbons and by the end of it, I have no idea what anyone on the street that day looked like. The piece of paper shows several Neanderthals wearing grey clothes and earmuffs. I don't think any of them had earmuffs.

"And is there anything else you remember?" asks Inspector Khan.

We run through it all again. What I saw, where I saw it. The kidnapping, who I've told, who I haven't, the body on the shoreline. How Peter Romero looked, the gun, the bus.

"Big – tall, strong – with red curly hair and really angry."

Inspector Khan writes it in his little book.

"How are they – at home? My phone doesn't work down here and they're not very good at e-mail. Can I ring them from the landline?" I ask.

"Don't," says Inspector Khan. "If you can bear not to. Just in case."

"Oh," I say, trying to ignore the tears that are catching me by surprise. "But they're all OK – aren't they?"

"Perfectly safe, police living on site."

There's a long silence. Inspector Khan looks at

Helen. Helen looks back at Inspector Khan.

"Sergeant Lewis will go off duty now, and Sergeant Hughes will take over," says Helen. "Just in case."

I wish they'd all stop saying: *just in case*.

"Well, I think that's about it then," says Inspector Khan, standing. He walks towards the door. Helen picks up her boots and follows him. I can see from here that the back of his beautiful suit is covered in dog hair. And then he turns. "Maya – did you see anything else? Was there – anything else that maybe the camera didn't pick up? Any other object?"

I shake my head, because there wasn't. Was there? "Why?"

"Nothing," he says, his hand on the front door. "It's nothing."

# Chapter 16

All night I listen to the sounds of the house and the yard. From time to time the ponies stamp their feet on the stable floor and after a while I get used to it. Policemen come and go, sometimes inside, sometimes out. But the sounds I'm listening for are vehicles, distant, or footsteps, close.

I imagine the red-haired man wandering through the outbuildings, just out of sight, and then I remember the thickness of the door. The shuttered windows. The massive walls. The tall gates being the only way in. It is a fortress.

I wish I had the rabbit.

I wish I had Zahra.

Before dawn, I look at my phone again.

No signal, no messages.

I type: *Missing you,* to Zahra.

*Message failed to send.*

I wish I had the pictures. What did the inspector mean? What else does he think I saw?

I switch on my tablet and try to make a Wi-Fi connection. Google loads *really* slowly so I leave it on the chest of drawers and go downstairs – but I'm hoping I've beaten Ollie to what little Internet there is.

Two of the dogs don't move, but Megan comes over and sniffs at my bare feet.

Auntie V is standing in the kitchen in her nightie, dressing gown and huge felt slippers. "You're up early," she says. She grabs a load of horrible meaty innards and jams them in a saucepan. "Giblets. For the dogs," she says as explanation before slapping it on to the stove.

The house fills with the fug of boiling offal and I retreat to the bedroom.

Slow dawn light filters through the window and I peer out expecting to see the red-headed man at any moment. But all I see is grey. It's snowed overnight. The grey fades to white. Icing sugar coats the mountains and the walls.

My tablet has loaded at last and I type in *Georgio Romero*. And then the Wi-Fi dies.

Rats!

This must be why Ollie's so good at horse riding. There's nothing else to do around here.

Slow curls of snow blow past the window and I realise that it's suddenly started to fall quickly. Thickly. Through it, I see the police four-by-four arrive, pick someone up and set off up the track.

As I get dressed, the phone rings downstairs. I open my door so that I can hear Auntie V. There's someone there this time. She doesn't say much but I can hear the worry in her voice.

"Goodness – how awful. Last night? Are you sure they're connected?"

There's a long silence.

"We will – I will. Should I tell her?"

Another silence.

"OK, I won't if you don't think so. And thank you – having Sergeant Lewis back here would be a great relief."

I creep down the stairs. I hear her replace the phone in the cradle, and she turns the radio on so that she's singing along to some weird piece of opera by the time I enter the kitchen.

"Oh Maya," she says, too cheerfully. "Now, later on, Gethin, Ollie's friend from the next valley, is coming over to ride. Sergeant Hughes has gone home for a nap and a change of clothes but Sergeant Lewis will be back with us soon. But for now, can I get you some bacon and eggs?"

"Um," I say. "Just the eggs perhaps?"

"Stupid me, of course," she says. "Just the eggs."

* * *

I'm still wondering what it was that Auntie V heard on the phone when Ollie's friend arrives.

"Gethin lives in Ty Fach, on the other side of the mountain, where Helen the policewoman comes from," Auntie V says. "There are so few of us up here, and so far apart that it's like a village spread over hundreds of square miles."

She puts bacon on plates, then remembers that I don't eat it, and gets a new plate.

"So I come over when I can," says Gethin. "Always have done."

"Yes, Gethin's always over here." Auntie V lands a grilled tomato on my plate. It slides sideways, slopping into my lap.

"Ah!" I yelp, trying to pick it up but burning my fingers.

"Oh God! Sorry," says Auntie V, rushing for a fish slice.

"Princess and the tomato," says Ollie, "the fairy tale they didn't write."

"The princess thing's wearing a bit thin, Ollie," I say.

Ollie snorts and wipes his mouth with the back of his hand. Gethin keeps a straight face and Auntie V lowers her head so that I can't see.

The phone rings. Ollie answers it.

"Hello – Valley Trekking—" he says.

He listens.

"Hello? Ow!"

He holds the phone away from his ear. "That really hurt," he says.

"Good," I say under my breath.

"What is it?" asks Gethin.

"It whistled at me, now it's clicking. It happened a couple of times yesterday," says Ollie.

"I think you should report a fault," says Gethin like an adult.

"I would but just at the moment we're not allowed to bring attention to ourselves or the house," Ollie swings round to stare at me. "Because of HER."

Part of me says I shouldn't answer – but the other part is getting angrier. "Sorry," I say. "I didn't ask to be here – stuck in the middle of nowhere."

"Why *are* you here?" asks Gethin. "Sorry," he says. "I don't mean that rudely."

"She's hiding from a red-haired man," says Ollie. "Who hangs around in Regent Street, attacking people."

"What?" says Gethin.

"He's got a gun!" I say.

"Who? Why?" asks Gethin.

"It's complicated," I say.

"Hush, hush, top secret," says Ollie, slapping the side of his nose with a grubby finger. "She's a protected witness or something."

"Really?" asks Gethin.

Auntie V stops bustling and listens, her back to the counter.

They're all staring at me.

"OK," I begin. "So there was this bloke, Georgio Romero, who got pulled out of the Thames. I saw his dead body, actually." I glare at Ollie. "And it's his brother, Peter, who's after me – I saw him pull a gun on a woman in Regent Street. And the police think he shot Georgio."

"Oh!" Gethin raises his eyebrows.

"Google him," I say. "Go on."

"May I?" asks Gethin, pulling over Ollie's laptop and furiously typing.

We sit in silence watching the circle spin.

Eventually, up comes a murky black and white image, which might be a person, might be a sheep.

"That's him?" says Gethin, pointing at the screen.

I nod. Even a screen seems too close.

"But why does he want you? You didn't see the actual murder – did you?"

I shake my head. "No – that's what's so weird – I don't know why he wants me, but the police think he does."

"You must have seen something else – something important, can you remember?"

"Huh!" says Ollie. "It's all stupid."

I try really hard to let his words go over my head but I can't. "OK, that's it!" I say. "Just stop it, Ollie. It's not as if I want to be here, stuck in the back of beyond in your smelly bedroom." It begins to flow. "But I'm not intending to hang about for long, murderer or no murderer, and then you can have it back and stare up at your boring mountain to your heart's content. Maybe while you wait for your rubbish Wi-Fi to actually bother to connect you to civilisation. Then you'll never have to see me again and I can forget all about you and your appalling manners."

"Ha!" Ollie stands so that he's leaning right over the breakfast table. "I didn't like you when you came all those years ago, with your little white socks and perfect hair. Scared of horses, scared of the doggie, always crying to Mummy and whining on and on." He raises his voice, his breath is making my fringe flap. "And I don't like you now. You, from your perfect stupid family, coming here like you own the place. Like you can just invade MY LIFE. Rearranging my bedroom, complaining that you can't get on the Internet, as if the world will stop turning if you can't get your stupid e-mails from your stupid friends. And endlessly poking at the food that's put in front of you, as if it's been scraped off your shoe—"

"Ollie!" shouts Auntie V, going bright red.

"Gosh," says Gethin and looks at me.

"If it makes you feel any better," I say, boiling fury racing over my scalp, "I didn't exactly take to you either – I seem to remember finding slugs in my shoes? Salt in my ice cream?"

Ollie smirks.

"And there was an evil dog that bit me, and you were SO rude – just like you are now, and no matter how angry you are, no matter how inferior I make you feel, about whatever you're angry about, that's no excuse for being so horrible. You have no idea how terrifying it is to have a man with a gun looking for you. I'm scared, because there's some madman after me! He kidnapped my sister, for goodness' sake – how badly must he want me? I'm scared for my family in London, and I'm feeling every scrap of your, your whatever – don't you understand? I don't want to be here. I'd rather be in London with my friends, I'd rather be enjoying the end of the Christmas term with parties and FUN, not stuck here in your – stables with stupid horses and hay and soup and bothering your mother because I'm a vegetarian – I didn't do it on purpose you know, it's happened. And you have no idea what it feels like."

There's a massive silence.

Gethin and Auntie V look back to Ollie.

"God, you're such a townie," he says, leaning back in his chair.

"What?" I say. He is *unbelievable!*

"Bet you can't even ride."

"What?" I say again. Then, "Of course I can ride!" A blush races up my throat.

"Can you?" Ollie leans forward, bumping the front legs of his chair back on to the floor. "Can you really?"

"Yes," I say, so angry I'd say anything.

"Go on, then," says Ollie. "Prove it."

# Chapter 17

Half an hour later and I'm still shaking with fury.

"I really think this is a bad idea," says Auntie V as Ollie leads a mean-looking black pony from the stables into the yard. "And I'm not sure Samson's right for Maya, either."

"She says she can ride," says Ollie. "If she can ride, she can ride Samson."

Auntie V catches me by the elbow. "Maya — don't."

"I'm fine, Auntie V," I say. "Bit of fresh air is just what I need, I've been dying to get back in the saddle."

Bundling the reins in my left hand, I eye the pony. And the pony eyes me back. There's something about that look, and when it tries to bite me, I realise Ollie's chosen it on purpose.

I can't remember how to mount. I glance towards Ollie, but he's already in the saddle. Damn. I know I need to be facing backwards to get on. Gethin holds the stirrup out for me and points towards my left foot. I stick my foot in the stirrup and do something supreme with my legs and stomach muscles and even as Samson takes a step forward, I hoist myself up so that I am almost standing on my left foot. I feel a hand on my bum and suddenly I am up there, swinging over the saddle, pointing the right way, hauling the reins up and thrashing about with my right leg to find the other stirrup.

Samson bends around and nibbles the toe of my boot.

"Hmm," says Auntie V.

Gethin leaps lightly into his own saddle, and Samson makes a lunge for his pony's backside, but Gethin skilfully steers out of the way and trots ahead out of the yard.

"Right," I say, gathering my reins the way Gethin

did and Samson stands, waiting.

Turning, Ollie puts his fingers to his mouth and lets out a loud whistle. Samson springs awake, jerks up his head and follows.

So that's how it is. Here am I, riding the pony equivalent of Ollie up a mountain with someone who hates me at the controls.

Really perfect.

Ollie leads, Gethin goes in the middle and I bobble along at the back, as the snow intensifies.

We pick our way up the lower track between the high walls in a silent line of three. I feel stupid and vulnerable.

What is it Granddad says? *Act in haste, repent at leisure.* Never really understood it before, but I think I do now.

Ollie whistles again, and two of the dogs appear behind us. One of them might be Megan.

A crow takes off from behind a wall and Samson skitters to the side.

I manage to stay on.

Not smug. But quietly confident.

But a little later Samson succeeds in blowing my cover.

I'm not sure what he does, but I think it involves

teeth, and Gethin's pony's bum, and then a kick in the face. But one moment I'm sitting on an almost motionless horse in a snowstorm. The next, I'm hurtling across the field towards a stone wall, clinging to Samson's neck.

"Stop!" I yell, frantically pulling on the reins.

"Pull harder, stop him!" shouts Gethin.

The thought that Samson could actually jump the wall is quickly pushed aside by the idea that he might just crash into it.

He slows and in that second I jump from the saddle, my feet thumping over the soggy grass, dragging on the reins.

Samson tries to stop, but he's still moving faster than me, and I feel his skull hitting my jaw, hear a crunch in my head, taste blood in my mouth.

I grip the bridle. Hanging on, digging my heels into the muddy grass, skidding sideways and downwards, I wait for the world to stop turning. Dragging downwards until Samson stops, trembling and blasting steam through his nostrils into my face.

* * *

I get back on. I haven't really got a choice.

Gethin's sympathetic.

Ollie's just silent. It's as if he's stopped being rude, but he still can't say anything nice.

I swallow the blood, bite back the tears and swear at Samson. He immediately tries to take another swipe at Gethin's horse.

"Stupid creature," I say, to the blizzard.

"Come on, Gethin!" yells Ollie.

Samson speeds up and I cling on. It's really uncomfortable and the snow stings the bruises on my face – although Samson is like sitting on a hot-water bottle and I kind of like the way we're moving over the ground, just the sound of his hooves slicing through the squeaky snow.

Both the dogs trot to the front, disappearing into the snow, it's so deep.

My phone pings, but there's no way I'm going to look at it until I'm firmly on the ground. If I drop it, it'll be lost until spring.

"You OK?" asks Gethin. Then he mutters, "You can't ride, can you?"

"No," I say. "But don't tell him that."

"I won't."

"Thanks," I say, brushing snow from my legs. "He doesn't like me very much, and nor does Samson."

"Both of them'll come round..." says Gethin, "...in the end. Give Ollie time. He's all right, really. He's having a bit of a hard time with his dad at the moment. He keeps making promises to visit and then lets him down at the last minute. Anyway, look on the bright side – isn't it great riding in the snow?"

\* \* \*

We climb up and up, following one behind the other. Soon we come upon the wall that the sheep ought to be behind.

At first it all looks white and then I spot the sheep crammed under a broken sheet of corrugated iron at the far end.

Their wool is almost black against the fresh snowfall and they've poked small holes through to the skimpy grass underneath. The ones that don't look up are digging with their hooves. They all look hungry.

"Where's the hay?" asks Gethin, swinging down from his pony and landing knee-deep in the white.

Ollie points at a huge pile of snow to the left of the track. "There's a shed with emergency stuff under there. We'll have to dig it out."

He drops from his horse, and pulls two folding shovels from a saddlebag. He chucks one at Gethin, and wades towards the mountain.

"Hey – what about me? I can dig."

He shrugs, but doesn't look at me.

"You're welcome to have a go with mine," says Gethin.

"No thanks," I say, touching the corner of my mouth where Samson clouted it. It's not bleeding any more, but it throbs.

Samson pricks his ears, listening.

I listen too.

Birdsong, sheep and an engine?

I can't see a thing and it occurs to me that anyone in a white suit of any sort would be invisible. Even one of those decorating overalls we sell in the shop. They could be really close. Within fifty metres, and we wouldn't know. We wouldn't see or hear them and Samson's black. He shows up quite well.

In my pocket, my phone buzzes. I watch Samson's ears swivelling back and forth and then he shakes his head and looks into the middle distance across the valley. He feels sprung.

Both the boys are digging. Leaning forward, I slip uncomfortably to the ground. The snow is surprisingly densely packed, so I don't get as low as Samson's hooves, which makes him seem quite small. I pat his neck and he swipes his head around, just catching the sleeve of my fleece with his teeth.

"No," I say, firmly, and much to my surprise he lets go.

Underneath the phone, I find the bag of liquorice. I slip my fingers in and take out a piece, slipping it into my mouth. Samson looks at me. Accusingly.

"You want some?" I ask.

He obviously isn't going to answer, except with his teeth, so I take a piece from the bag, and flatten my hand completely to let him take it.

He doesn't grab it, instead he picks it gently from my hand, curling his lips around the little black stick and chewing it experimentally.

I check the phone. A message from Zahra, sent yesterday.

*There's been hit-and-run in Llandovery (that's really near you). They think Peter Romero was driving the car. TAKE CARE. X*

I fumble with my phone, my fingers thick and slow with the cold.

*When?* I ask her.

*Yesterday,* comes back immediately.

I stare at the message.

Llandovery?

We passed it on the way here.

This must be what Auntie V was told this morning.

So he *is* here. He's been watching me since I arrived. But where? Right by us at the top of the mountain? Or down by the farm? I stare into the blizzard. I really can't see anything.

By the shed, Ollie straightens up and stares in the same direction as Samson.

"Helicopter," he says.

The boys both stare into the snow.

The dogs raise their heads to listen.

"If we can't see anything, then neither can anyone else," says Gethin.

For a second, I feel paralysed.

"Let me have a go with that shovel," I say in the end, and grabbing it off Ollie, I grit my teeth and drive at the snow, matching Gethin load for load and revealing the shed door.

After about two minutes, I lower the shovel. Ollie is watching me and I can't work out his expression. The bottom of my back aches, so I straighten up, stretch and then resume digging. I wonder if he's surprised to see me, his princessy London cousin, dig.

"Here," says Gethin, handing his shovel to Ollie. "I need a break."

Ollie steps over and quickens the rate. I now find myself digging faster than I was before, because I can't possibly let him get there first.

My hands hurt, my back hurts, and actually, my feet are starting to freeze even though the rest of me is boiling.

"Stop!" calls Gethin. "What are you doing? You could easily open the doors now – look."

He's completely right, and Ollie and I step back. I don't look at Ollie and I'm pretty sure Ollie doesn't look at me. Neither of us wants to give in.

We pull open the doors. There's almost no hay.

"What?" says Ollie. "But I thought there was supposed to be loads. The sheep won't survive up here without it and this snow's going to last days."

"We'll have to go back down, get the Land Rover and drive up with some," says Gethin.

"Or bring the sheep down, a few at a time?" I suggest.

"The Land Rover won't make it. The snow's too deep," says Ollie.

And then I have a thought.

# Chapter 18

The horses cover the ground surprisingly fast, keeping us to the right of the path, for good reason. To our left is a precipice, a sharp drop that seems to go on forever. The snow comes down harder than before and the wind blows wilder, and I feel quite safe. I can hardly see Gethin or his pony.

The dogs have completely disappeared.

I realise as we approach that the thing I took to be a split in the mountain-top is actually a road between two piles of slate. And that the actual top of the mountain is a spoil heap.

Samson stops in the middle of the quarry and

blows steam from his nostrils. The boys both slide to the ground and leave their ponies standing.

It's weirdly quiet in here. Everything echoes, everything's louder. It's shaped like a horseshoe with a narrow entrance and a big circular middle. To the right are four little trucks, like miniature railway trucks. They must be the things that used the rails I found yesterday.

"So, M'ilady — what's the plan?" says Ollie, standing back, his arms folded across his chest.

Annoying or what?

I slide down from Samson. The boys watch as I wander over to the lump that's covered by a tarpaulin. Gethin helps me tug it off, sending snow cascading to the ground and the ponies scuttling to the far side of the quarry.

Underneath is the bulldozer. Smaller than I expected, and greyer. I'm aware that even the ponies are watching me, so I try to look really unconcerned and really knowledgeable. Actually, it's not remotely like the motorbikes I've worked on before, it's all huge and the metal's corroded with rust. But I can see the clean shiny bits that Ollie has done, and the orange rusty bits that he hasn't. I can also see where he's oiled it, and where he's greased it. I feel excited. This looks as if it ought to work.

Actually, it kind of has to.

For my sake, and for the sheep.

"And where's the trailer?" I ask.

"You're mad," says Ollie.

"Fine, I'm mad, but I just want to try it," I say.

"It won't work."

"Humour me," I say, echoing my mum.

*** 

"So – have you got the key?" I say.

He points at the ignition. "S'there."

"OK – can we try starting it?" I say.

Ollie sighs and clambers up to the seat.

There's a clunk and nothing more.

"See?" he says. "It won't work."

I think about what Granddad said.

"I know it sounds stupid, but can you have another go? Hold the key in the starting position. I want to try something."

Ollie shrugs, turns the key, and I take a large icy spanner from the side, and hit the fuel pump.

"What're you doing?" he shouts. "Don't smash her up!"

"Don't worry," I say. "I'm not – I just..." I clunk

the spanner against the fuel pump, slightly harder this time, and there's the faintest cough from deep inside the engine.

Ollie jumps and the whole machine judders with an extraordinary noise – a puff of black smoke spurting out of the vertical exhaust pipe by his leg.

"Wow!" he shouts. "Wow!"

The ponies panic and stamp at the back of the quarry.

"I'll get them," says Gethin, and he magically calms them, walking them back out towards the blizzard. "I'll meet you by the sheep."

"So do you know how to drive it?" I shout at Ollie.

"Dunno," he says, swinging the long gearstick round and gripping the steering wheel.

The engine thud becomes deeper and growlier and the bulldozer inches forward. The machine rattles and groans but it doesn't fall apart. I step back and stand against the pile of slate on the other side. I do hope Ollie knows how to stop.

He does. And he knows how to go backwards too.

And forwards.

And backwards.

And forwards.

It leaves flattened, rust-spattered, oily fingers of ice moulded into inverse images of the tracks.

Slowly, slowly, Ollie inches away from the wall until the bulldozer sits right in the middle of the quarry, facing out into the blizzard. He's got a huge grin on his face although when he catches my eye, he straightens his face and looks serious again.

"Let's get the trailer," I shout over the engine.

"Right," Ollie shouts back. He fiddles with something by his leg and leaves the bulldozer chugging gently by itself.

"C'mon, it's over here," he says, moving towards another vast pile of snow.

We tug at the tarpaulin, which is ridiculously heavy under the snowfall. At first all I can see is an enormous tyre, with something wooden and blue on top. And then, when we've pulled the cover off completely I see what Auntie V meant by a trailer.

It's really a sort of farm cart, four huge wheels, with tractor tyres. Tall sides and a tailgate. Ollie clambers up on top and chucks down the last corner of tarpaulin.

"It doesn't have a brake, but it was obviously built to be pulled by the bulldozer," he says.

"Wow," I say, staring at it. "We'll never pull it over to connect it though."

"Don't have to," he says. "We'll bring the bulldozer to it."

"OK," I say. "If you think so."

I'm sure it *is* possible to back a mini bulldozer within a couple of centimetres of a trailer. I've even seen it done on YouTube, but when Ollie does it, the corner of the trailer ends up a bit flatter than it was before.

"Rats," he says, getting down to inspect the damage. "That's sixty years old that trailer." But surprisingly he doesn't throw a tantrum.

We pull a metal loop across and link it firmly to the tow bar on the back of the bulldozer.

Ollie stands back. "I never thought this would happen," he says, and he very nearly smiles at me, but catches himself at the last minute.

"Down to the sheep?" I shout into the wind.

He nods vigorously and climbs up into the seat.

The engine increases in intensity and the machine grinds forward, the trailer jolts, lurches and follows, rolling easily in the bulldozer's giant flattened tracks.

"Yee-hah!" shouts Ollie from the driving seat.

"Yay!" I yell into the wind.

Despite the bulldozer's size the quarry floor vibrates under my feet and I walk behind on the compressed snow watching as the trailer swings slightly from side to side, narrowly missing the wall to the left of the track but keeping well away from the precipice on the right. Ollie steers it out of the mine, flattening the drifted snow like candyfloss. The flakes of new snow melt easily on the engine.

It's easy to walk now, because everything's squashed and the chunks of icy snow ping sideways under my feet.

Ollie stops by the hay shed and climbs down. "Gethin's not here," he shouts. "He must have taken the horses back – probably just as well."

"Do you think we can get the sheep up into the trailer with the engine running?" I ask. "It's just the fuel-pump trick might not work twice."

"We can try," he says and we go over to peer at the sheep. They stare up at us.

"How are we going to get them up there?" Ollie asks. "I don't think I can lift them that high."

In answer, I open the door of the shed and check inside. Pallets. A stack of them, and some corrugated iron.

"We'll build a ramp," I say.

\* \* \*

You'd think the sheep would want to get out of the freezing cold and into a lovely clean specially prepared trailer. But no – sheep are not that intelligent. What they really want to do is race around in circles driving people mad and going nowhere.

We line the floor of the trailer with hay, we scatter hay up the ramp, we put a big blob of it in the middle of the trailer; we back the trailer into the entrance of the field. It's so obvious.

But the sheep won't play.

They run away into the snow, burrowing themselves like dirty cotton wool in clean cotton wool.

They stand and quiver until Ollie approaches, at which point they then rear and bolt.

"You stupid creatures," I shout into the wind.

The sheep turn to look and scatter in different directions.

All but one.

That sheep wrinkles its upper lip, teddy boy style, and wees long and yellow into the snow.

I grab it.

It pulls back, but the wool's well-attached to its back and my fingers are well-anchored in the wool.

"You, sheep," I say. "Are coming with me."

The sheep eyes me. I suspect it's sizing me up. "I can tell you now sheep that you can run faster and bite harder, but I'm not going to let go." I drag at the sheep's wool and like a resistant toddler, it slides across the snow — its legs locked straight.

It is actually quite heavy. I drag again, and this time it comes a little easier, leaving four leg-sized scratches in the snow. I get it to the entrance of the field, beside the trailer.

"This ..." I say, "... is hay." I hold a small bunch of it in front of the animal's nose.

"It is good to eat. You will enjoy it."

The sheep keeps its mouth firmly closed — its feet motionless. The snow settles on my hand embedded in the sheep's wool.

"You're supposed to walk up the ramp," I say, pointing into the trailer.

The sheep stays still.

"Perhaps," I say, thick flakes of snow landing on my eyelashes, "you want to die out here on this frozen hillside?"

The sheep pulls against me, but I don't let go.

Instead, I put my legs on either side of its body and march it up the creaking, juddering ramp. It's not really willing, but it's slightly less unwilling than it was before.

We reach the top of the ramp and I slither the sheep towards the sections of hay scattered across the floor of the trailer. It puts its head down and starts to eat, grabbing at the hay with the enthusiasm of a creature that hasn't eaten for twelve hours.

This is great. One sheep up, only twenty-something more to go.

I turn to see what the others are doing and to my surprise, they're sniffing around the bottom of our makeshift ramp. Behind them, Ollie holds a long stripy pole, and gives them gentle taps on their bottoms until they begin to advance. First one, then two, gallop up the slippery corrugated iron until they reach the top.

"Go on," he says, "keep going, girls."

Half the sheep are now at the top but I don't let go of mine. I can see that it works by getting one and the others will follow, but if I lose that one, then I could lose them all.

The last sheep clangs on to the ramp and Ollie practically pushes it up the slope, slamming the back of the trailer shut behind them.

"Thirty?" I call.

"Yes," he says. "Now we've just to get them back down the hill."

From up here, I look into the valley. It's invisible, just a white screen, whirling and swirling. My feet are so cold I can't feel them, and my fingers are going the same way. We've done the impossible. The bulldozer works and the sheep are in the trailer but we've still got to get them safely down.

"It's getting worse," I say, but I don't think Ollie can hear me over the sound of the engine. He pulls the corrugated iron away and checks the back of the trailer before pulling himself up into the driving seat.

"Should I stay in here?" I shout.

He holds a thumb up, so I crouch among the sheep, who nuzzle and tug at me as they try to stuff their bellies with hay.

The trailer lurches as we set off down the track but steadies quickly. I close my eyes and try to imagine it rolling neatly behind the bulldozer, instead of careering madly down the hill and tipping me and thirty sheep into a snowy ditch.

*Crump.*

I open my eyes. The bulldozer is still in front and we are still behind. A dented field entrance is also behind, but Ollie is driving really slowly, really carefully and it's looking great. We drop down past the highest fields. Ollie slows and I scramble down from the trailer to open the gate. He so nearly makes it through without damage, just twanging the metal of the gate and leaving it slightly bowed.

It almost shuts and I pull myself up again nestling among the sheep.

"Brilliant, sheep," I say. "We made it, we made it back down to the farm."

"Yee-hah!" shouts Ollie, which is when the trailer goes into an invisible pothole and tips me and most of the sheep out into the snow.

# Chapter 19

"What do you think you were doing?" asks Auntie
V, sticking antiseptic cream on to the ice-cut on
my nose.

"Rescuing the sheep," says Ollie.

"But with a bulldozer?" says Auntie V. "That's..."

"Brilliant," says Gethin, pouring hot milk into
mugs of cocoa. "Brilliant."

"Inspired," says Ollie. "Absolutely inspired.
You've no idea, Mum, just how bad the weather is
up there at the top of the hill. We'd have lost the
sheep."

"Sorry," I say. "Ow! I didn't think how much

damage the bulldozer would do to the gate."

Auntie V swings my chin up so that she can see right into my eyes. "It's not the *gateposts* I was worried about. The main thing is you're all back safe and sound. The sheep are safely tucked up in the hay barn, the ponies are safe, and we've now got our very own snowplough!"

* * *

Gethin's dad arrives in a tractor to take him home.

"There's still no policeman," I say. "I thought he'd be here by now."

"I passed some police just now, so they'll be with you in a minute, love," he says.

Ollie disappears up to his room. "Gonna change my trousers."

Auntie V goes out to the hay barn where the sheep are milling about. Alone downstairs, I ping open my phone and reread Zahra's messages.

She hasn't sent any more.

I grab my tablet and type *Llandovery* into the search engine, but the Wi-Fi's too weak and it soon reverts to the dinosaur. Ollie's right, it does seem to be supplied by Feeble dot com.

The early afternoon light slants through the kitchen window and I stand in the warmth holding my tablet, loading and reloading. On guard. Megan stands next to me, alert. We're both listening.

It would be really brilliant to see either Auntie V, or the police, or both, but the track stays empty. Behind me, the clock is maddening. The silence between ticks is vast.

A sound makes me looks up. A police four-by-four stops outside the gate. Two of the dogs race towards the door, Megan lowers herself to her haunches and growls.

"Hey, dogs," I say, "the cavalry's arrived."

\* \* \*

From the kitchen window I can see the back of the car. I'm expecting it to be Sergeant Lewis from yesterday, but it isn't — this man's bigger and he's wearing a beanie hat with "POLICE" embroidered across the front.

He skids out of the door of the car and leans back in to pick something up. As he does so, a single ginger curl springs from the side of his hat and catches in the watery sunlight.

Oh!

Oh, no!

"Ollie!" I yell.

"OLLIE!"

But Ollie doesn't come.

I'm frozen. I stand staring through the window, watching the man straighten up. He pushes the curl back under his hat and checks his face in the wing mirror.

It's him.

The clock on the wall ticks.

I hear the gate swing open, creaking.

Retreating from the window, I duck down and feel my heart beat in my eardrums.

I creep around to the front door. There's no key in the huge lock, but the bottom of the door has an ancient rusty bolt going straight down into the flagstone floor. With both hands I try to silently push it down, but I can't move it. It's solid. It obviously hasn't been used for years.

I try again, succeeding only in skinning my knuckles.

*Crunch, crunch.*

The man's footsteps pad on the ice crust in the yard, getting closer.

I could run upstairs or I could try to hold the door shut.

I grab the only weapon I can see. An old metal flat iron, and wedge the top of a chair under the door handle, balancing the iron above the door. Racing upstairs to Ollie's room, I hammer on the door.

"He's here – we need to hide."

"What are you on about?" He's sitting on his bed in a T-shirt and underpants.

"The murderer, Peter Romero, he's here. We have to hide," I gabble. "There must be somewhere. Show me."

Dazed, he stands and looks around. "There should be a torch here, there's a priest's hole under the stairs." On top of a pile of *What Car?* magazines I spot a head-torch, grab it and race towards the top of the stairs.

"Where?" I say.

Downstairs, the dogs are going bonkers, and I can hear heavy knocking on the door. There's a crashing sound.

"Here," says Ollie, pushing an embroidered hanging to one side and opening a tiny doorway. "Quick. You first."

I throw myself into the tiny space expecting a floor and find it a couple of metres lower than I thought. Cobwebs brush my face and the square of light above me disappears as Ollie crams into the space alongside.

"Will the hanging cover the door again?" I whisper.

"Hope so," he mutters.

*Clunk.* That'll be the iron falling from the front door.

Heavy feet sound on the flagstones.

Ollie and I go completely still.

The feet clump on the stairs.

We sit in a tiny pool of torchlight, listening.

The cold bleeds into my legs. Colder than I've ever been.

In here, the thumps are muffled. I realise we must be within the walls of the downstairs of the house and although we probably can't be heard we both stay silent.

I play the torch around the walls. They're made of huge damp blocks of rock, coloured with strange yellow lichens. It's a dungeon.

A prison.

If someone shoots us down here, no one will ever know.

Boards thump and the dogs bark. Then there are more heavy footsteps on the stairs and the floorboards over our head creak.

The creaking stops.

Starts again.

"He's in your bedroom," whispers Ollie.

My heart beats so loudly I have to cover my ears to hear the silence.

He's in there for ages, and then the feet sound again.

Something heavy slides across the floor.

I turn off the torch and we sit in the dark, listening.

There's a really long silence in which I wonder if he can see the door. I imagine him pulling back the hanging and seeing it.

I hold my breath, just like I do when I'm playing hide-and-seek with the twins and Zahra.

Ollie holds his.

Feet sound on the boards again, disappearing a little before reappearing on the stairs behind us.

I feel Ollie tense up beside me and I reach my hand over to his. "Wait," I whisper.

The dogs bark in the house. I can't work out if he's gone or is still there, hoping we'll come out.

We wait.

# Chapter 20

"I'm so sorry," says Sergeant Lewis. "I should have been here, but I had to pick up a prescription for Mrs Preston. It only took a minute but..."

Auntie V gives him a worried look. "Just as well you got back when you did," she says.

"I know, the moment I saw that car outside the yard I knew there was something wrong." He pours himself another cup of tea. "But I'd no idea ... he's a big man, isn't he? Knocked me right over on the way out."

He goes to stand outside the front door and I wonder just how much use he is.

Ollie sits next to me on the sofa.

"That was terrifying," he says.

"Yes," I say, resisting the desire to say: now you know what I feel.

Ollie stares into the fire and then jumps to his feet. "Stay there," he says and rushes out into the yard.

The flames leap and fall as Ollie crashes back in through the front door and a small wet thing lands in my lap.

Rabbit.

"Oh!"

"I saw it, yesterday, in the snow. It's yours, isn't it?"

I nod, biting back a tiny sentimental tear. "Thanks, thank you."

"Should have picked it up before," he mumbles, leaning forward to toast his hands at the front of the wood burner. I think that's a kind of apology.

"He was in the house, Mum, that man was in our house."

Auntie V shivers. "I know. And they haven't caught him."

\* \* \*

Snow falls ever harder, and Inspector Khan rings

140

from London.

"You're to stay in," he says. "We've got people on all entry and exit roads, and the house is under surveillance from up the mountain."

"I can't go out at all?"

"No. Not even into the yard. You must stay in the house. But now that he definitely knows you're there, I think you can ring your family. Maybe give it a couple of hours. Anyway, we've removed the phone taps."

"So the phone *was* tapped?"

There's a silence. "Um – yes," he says. "We think he's been listening in, trying to find out any plans."

"Is that how he found me? Through the phone?"

He pauses. "We don't think so, no. Could he have followed you on to that bus? Is that possible?"

I remember the bus. Stopping and starting all the way down the road. It was packed.

"He might have done," I say. "And what about the hit-and-run in Llandovery?"

"You know about that?"

I stay silent.

"We're assuming it was Peter Romero because it was his brother's car."

"But why is he after me? I still don't understand."

"He must think you saw more than you did. That's why it would be really helpful to know what you saw, even if you don't think it's significant. You understand?"

I nod at the phone. I understand.

*　*　*

Keeping away from the windows, I crawl across the floor and sit in a dark patch by the wood burner where I reckon no bullet could ever reach. I can't prove what I saw, but perhaps I can work out what I might be searching my memory for.

I google Romero.

The loading circle turns and turns and nothing happens.

I look across at Ollie, staring at his laptop. I know that he's also watching a loading circle, waiting for contact with the outside world.

He glances up at me. He doesn't smile, but he doesn't frown. Perhaps hiding from a murderer under the stairs has changed his view. That and my bulldozer cure. And he did give me the rabbit.

Perhaps, if I ask nicely, he'll give up his little scrap of Wi-Fi so that I can actually look up something important, because if I'm going to be imprisoned like this then I need to know more about the Romeros.

It's worth trying.

"Ollie," I say. "Could we look up some stuff on your laptop?" And although it feels really hard to ask, I say, "Would you help me with this?"

Dropping a cushion to the floor next to me, he sits with his laptop on his knees.

"Go on then," he says. "Shoot."

I look at him.

"OK – bad choice of words. Tell me what you know."

I gaze at him to check that he's one hundred per cent serious about this, and decide that he is. The stupid competitive Ollie seems to have been replaced by something almost human.

"I don't know much, but can we look up *Peter Romero*."

Ollie types it in and we both gaze at the screen. I'm thinking about us hiding in the priest's hole. I'm thinking of Romero holding a gun inches away from me on the other side of the front door. I'm thinking that something doesn't quite make sense.

*Peter Romero* loads. There are six hits.

Eventually, there are some smiling pictures of random Americans. One beaming at the camera in

143

golf gear, another aged five in a pair of swimming trunks and two Spanish-looking men with a canoe.

"There," I say, pointing at the bottom of the screen. Three pictures. Two are blurry portraits. We look up the sites they're on and they link to the newspaper articles. They seem to come from a CCTV camera.

"Keep trying," I say and Ollie clicks down the entries.

"Bingo," he says.

It's a wedding. A bride and groom who I don't recognise and then my man standing behind them, smiling. Looking good in a suit.

Ollie clicks on the picture. It leads to a wedding photographer's site in London. It has the picture, and the names of the people in the photo underneath.

"Tracey Torofdar and Sam Pridham," reads Ollie.

"Look them up," I say.

There's a Tracey Torofdar who works for a mobile-phone company.

And a Sam Pridham who works for a London art auctioneer, in theft recovery.

I stare at the wall.

And then back at the picture.

"Why would he shoot his brother?" I say. "I can't imagine it. It's so alien. He must be a monster. But he doesn't look like a monster. He doesn't look like a killer."

"What does a killer look like?" asks Ollie.

"I don't know, I suppose I've never seen one," I say. "Except for him."

Outside the wind batters the house and new snow taps on the windows. I wonder how close Peter Romero is. He could be just outside the farm, hiding in the snow. He could be watching the gate from somewhere up on the mountain.

Headlights shine in the yard and I tense up, before realising it's just the police patrol checking on Sergeant Lewis.

He sticks his head around the door. "Both of us now you'll be glad to hear. Me and WPC Catherine Jones."

"Good," says Auntie V. "Coffee?"

"That'd be lovely," says the sergeant, disappearing out into the hall.

"What exactly does Peter Romero do?" I ask, as Ollie types the name in again and flicks through masses of entries. "I mean – most people are on some sort of register for work."

"He doesn't appear to do anything," says Ollie.

He clicks on a link that looks promising before it vanishes. Just vanishes.

"What?" he says. "Where's it gone?"

He clicks back and forth and then it just says, *unauthorised*.

We stare at the screen.

"That's odd," he says. "It's like he doesn't exist."

"There's a lot about this that doesn't make sense. Can you look for the newspaper article about Georgio?"

Ollie works back through the tabs until he finds it.

While we wait for the article to load, Megan comes over and lays her head on my knee. It's heavy, but curiously comforting.

*Some years ago he was associated with the theft of a very small Vermeer painting from a private collection, but charges were dismissed.*

Ollie types in: *Art theft + Romero.*

Some old articles come up, one connecting Georgio with a missing Matisse, stolen from a private collection in Denmark, and another one mentioning his part in the return of a painting stolen from a museum in Italy.

*He is also thought to be connected to a Vermeer stolen in 2001 by a European gang from an exhibition in the Netherlands.*

There's a picture of it. It's two girls standing in a kitchen. *Girls in Kitchen*, it says.

"Gah!" says Ollie sitting back. "We're going round in circles. And anyway, that inspector from London must know twice what we know."

I hate to admit it, but he's right.

Handing me the laptop, he clambers back up off the floor and stretches out on the sofa, staring up at the ceiling.

The fire spits and crackles. The wind lifts the heavy curtain hanging over the hall door and I shiver. I know that the snow must be falling and falling. I wonder if they'll ever get Peter Romero? He's got the whole of Wales to hide in.

Auntie V switches on the telly.

Antiques Roadshow. They're talking about a painting of a cow. "Twenty thousand pounds at auction, possibly..." says the expert.

The woman who owns the painting pretends to be surprised and the camera moves on to a hideous dog-shaped jug, that's worth a fiver.

I close my eyes and try really hard to remember

what it was I saw in Regent Street. People on the pavement, rushing. The lights, the coats and shopping bags and faces, lots of faces. *Millions* of faces, and then the man at the back, the break in the crowd, him shouting at the woman, him holding the gun with one hand – and his other hand doing what?

Idly, I use Ollie's laptop to look up that Vermeer that was stolen in 2001. The private collection is unnamed, but in a small *Telegraph* article it suggests that it might belong to the Queen.

It was, is, very small. 21 × 24 centimetres. Smaller than a sheet of A4 paper. Painted possibly in 1664. Estimated value: two hundred million dollars.

What?

Is that two hundred *million*?

Auntie V gets a jar from a cupboard and pops the lid open. "Olives anyone?" she asks.

"Yes please," says Ollie.

"Good, good," she says, and then, glancing out of the window she says. "That snow's getting worse."

"Hmm," I agree.

Two hundred million.

"Really?" I say out loud.

"What?" says Ollie, hanging his head down from

the side of the sofa so that he's upside down.

"There's a painting here that's worth loads," I say. "And I'm sure it's connected, but I don't know how."

"Lay the table for me, Maya love, will you?" asks Auntie V.

I put the laptop down, and try to bring my head back to the here and now.

# Chapter 21

The snow is falling even harder now. All the mud has disappeared, the barn has disappeared. Everything has disappeared. Even the window has nearly disappeared.

"Goodness," says Auntie V. "I hope those policemen are all right."

Auntie V flicks through the channels. Shots of lorries skewed sideways on motorways and sheep stranded on hillsides fill the screen.

The phone rings and Auntie V rushes to pick it up. "You have? Oh! That's marvellous. Marvellous news."

She listens.

"We'll have them in for a cup of tea, and – yes – an hour or so. Quite. Well if necessary we can lend them the quad bike."

She puts the phone down.

"They've caught him. Heat-seeking helicopters found him on the other side of the mountain. He's been living there in a white tent, apparently. What a relief."

She smiles and in her eyes I see tears. I think she's been as scared as me, but trying to hold it together. Her, stuck on a mountainside with two children and a killer on the loose.

I sink into the sofa. Close my eyes and relax. I nearly fall asleep but Auntie V calls in Sergeant Lewis and WPC Jones and shoves pizza under our noses.

\* \* \*

Before bed, I ring Mum. She already knows.

"I'll try to come tomorrow, but having seen the pictures on the telly I can't see the van managing the motorway, let alone those lanes. Oh, it will be lovely to have you home, love – I've really missed you."

"I've really missed you too," I say, and I change

the screen saver on my tablet to a picture of the whole family standing together on Brighton beach.

I leave the curtains open. The light from the stable shines on my ceiling showing the soft silhouettes of snowflakes circling and circling.

Megan comes to sleep on the floor. I don't throw her out.

Sleep comes in doses.

In the middle of the night, an e-mail manages to come through. It's from Zahra, with loads of pictures of the party. And I fall asleep, replying. Feeling almost normal.

* * *

In the morning, the snow's still falling hard. So hard, I only catch glimpses of the stables. There's no way Mum's going to get here so I clamber out of bed, pull my clothes on and go downstairs.

"Can I make a snowman?" I ask.

"Oh, of course, Maya — I suppose snow means something quite different to you — it's just, we have to clear the lane in case anything happens to any of the horses and we need a vet."

"I'll do it with the bulldozer," says Ollie. "It'll only take a second."

We go out into the snow. It's floating thickly

from the sky, the mountain's gone, the roofs have gone. Everything is thick and invisible. But it feels great to be outside without being afraid.

Ollie clambers up into the seat and I clunk the fuel pump with a spanner and he chugs out of the yard and up the track, squashing the snow out of the way and flinging it over the walls on either side. I walk behind in the tracks, enjoying the sight of the new snow falling on the cleared mud of the path.

I wish Zahra were here, she'd love it. Back home, they'll be watching the same snow falling and melting on the main road. It'll be black already, and unless someone walks to the South Bank, no chance of snowmen for them.

But I could at least build a snowman and take a picture.

I begin with a ball, and roll it on the untouched snow crusting the tops of the walls.

It takes a moment to be the size of a football and I drop it on the verge where it begins to flock up with thick snow, soon becoming as big as a gym ball.

It's so easy. There's so much of it.

Rolling the snowman's body into the yard, I park

it by the front door and begin to pack more ice around the bottom so that it doesn't move. I begin another ball, this time from the corner of the yard, and soon, I've got enough for a head.

Behind me, the bulldozer thunders along the lane, and I rush to prop the gate open. It rumbles into the yard and stops just past the gate. Ollie slips down.

"Neat!" he says, pointing at the snowman. "I'll find you some coal for the buttons."

I stare up at the twirling snow. It falls like marshmallows from the sky, settling softly on my face and also on my snowman, softening his contours and covering up the muddy bits. It's fantastic, I've never seen anything like it.

"Great," says Ollie, bunging the buttons on to the front. "And thanks," he says, not meeting my eye. "Thanks for getting the bulldozer going. It's – magic."

"You'll have to thank Granddad. He's the one. He knew what we needed to do. I asked him – via Zahra," I admit. "I only really know about motorbikes."

"He knows a lot about machinery then?" says Ollie, packing some more snow around the back of the snowman.

"Yeah, he reckons everything's fixable, and he never gives up."

Ollie looks at the ground and kicks at the snow. "Mum says we're very similar."

"You and Granddad?"

"Yes – she says we're both bloody-minded. That we're always trying to reinvent the wheel. That we don't stop when we should."

"Determined?"

"Yes," he says.

"Oh." It's my turn to kick at the snow. Ollie sounds as if he's describing me.

"I'd love to see him, but we're so far away, and he doesn't travel much – does he?"

"Not often," I say. "But I'm sure he'd enjoy your bulldozer – and you of course."

Ollie shrugs and digs out a broken riding hat to stick on top of the snowman. The snow falls around us and I'm fascinated by the way it moves until something prickles on my spine. I look up. I feel as if I'm being watched but there's nothing there, only the snowman.

I pull my bobble hat closer to my head and wander to the front door. As I take off my boots I look again. But there's no one.

* * *

"Pancakes anyone?" says Ollie when we get inside.

Auntie V smiles and ruffles Ollie's hair. "Thank you, love. I think there's a lemon somewhere." She hunts in the fridge.

We eat, and I feel oddly vulnerable without our policemen and even though I know it's all over I look up the Vermeer painting again.

"What's that?" asks Ollie peering over my shoulder.

"The painting. The stolen one."

"Very small," says Ollie.

Auntie V switches on the telly. More pictures of lorries struggling along roads.

M4 mostly closed.

M5 mostly closed.

We eat the pancakes.

And chocolate.

And more chocolate.

And Ollie banks the fire higher, and I think about paintings and Regent Street.

* * *

At first light, Ollie drives the bulldozer out of the farm and along the main road until all we can see is a trail of black smoke against the snow. An hour later he comes back.

"Done it!" he says. "We're connected up all the way down to the village. If your Mum comes later, she should be able to get through. Anyone should be able to get through."

# Chapter 22

"Maya, love, how are you? Granddad's not well," Mum gabbles down the phone at breakfast time.

"Good, I'm good," I say. "We're looking forward to seeing you. What's wrong with him?"

"Well, I may not be able to come," says Mum. "He's got a shocking cough."

"Oh, Mum," I say.

"He'll be fine, he's on antibiotics but he can't work, so I'm watching the twins *and* working in the shop."

"What about Dad?" I say. "Couldn't he come?"

"It's a nine-hour round trip, sweetie, and there's

all that snow – but we'll do it as soon as possible."

"Oh," I say. "But we've cleared the road so that you can get through."

I hear Mum's intake of breath and then she says, "Can I speak to Auntie V?" Her voice carries the faintest wobble.

"Course," I say, handing the phone over and swallowing hard. I grab a cushion and hug it tight, fighting back the tears.

* * *

Auntie V says that we have to exercise the ponies in the indoor school. "They'll go mad – they've been indoors for too long."

My puffa jacket is still sopping wet from snowman-building, so I put on my new parka and hope very much that the horsehair will brush off. I take the liquorice from the puffa jacket and bung it in my pocket. I've kept it with me whenever I'm outside, just in case we get stuck in the snow. Mum once told me about a man who survived a whole night snowed-in with only a packet of sweets to eat.

We ride the ponies one after the next. I get pretty expert at mounting and dismounting. I even learn to put on a bridle. When it comes to

Samson, Auntie V makes me trot, and then for one very magical moment, canter. I don't fall off and I don't get bitten, which goes some way towards compensating me for Mum not coming.

While I'm joggling around on horseback, I think about my gunman, Peter Romero. Presumably by now he's safely locked up somewhere and telling his story to Inspector Khan.

That should make me feel safe, so I don't quite understand why it doesn't. We put the ponies back in the pony shed and pull the doors across.

We come out into spiralling candyfloss snow.

Once again, my spine tingles and I get that feeling of being watched but when I turn around, there's no one but the snowman.

The house phone rings. Auntie V goes in to answer it, shouting back to Ollie. "You're going to have to move that thing, Ollie." She points at the bulldozer. "It's blocking the yard. Take it back up to the mine."

Ollie scrambles up into the seat and when I bash the fuel pump it starts up a second time. I watch from a distance as the bulldozer climbs relentlessly up the hill, flattening the already flattened snow, motoring easily over the tussocks and lumps of the track until it disappears in the whiteness.

I wander back to the house, checking the gateway and the track. I still feel watched.

The dogs wander out to see what the noise is about and Megan pricks her ears, as if she can smell something.

"You too?" I say, stepping quickly into the porch and kicking my boots off.

"Oh dear, Louisa – how dreadful – I'll come over," Auntie V is talking on the phone. "But I don't think I want to bring the Land Rover – I'll take the quad bike – it'll be quicker. Half an hour? Yup, yup, ring the vet anyway, just in case he can come."

She puts down the receiver.

"Blast," she says. "It would happen now."

"What?" I say.

"Delivering a foal. I tend to help with them if they're difficult or the vet can't get there. Over at Capel Dewi." She looks very serious. "I'm really sorry Maya, but I'm going to have to go."

"Fine," I say, not meaning it. "We'll be fine."

"Feed the dogs if I'm not back. I'm sure Ollie'll appreciate some help feeding the horses – I could be all night, it's a draught horse. Big."

"Fine," I say.

"Good."

I watch her scurry about, getting things together. She puts on an enormous coat and boots and dashes out into the yard. Then she rushes back into the house and kisses me on the top of the head. "Take care, Maya."

"Why?"

"It's all been rather – traumatic hasn't it? And I'm sure you'd love to be at home, back in that cosy flat with all the noise and bustle." She looks sad for a millisecond before stepping out into the snow. A moment later there's a bang and some smoke and she emerges from a shed on a small rusty-red quad bike. She waves and bounces off along the track, trailing smoke and snow.

The house goes quiet and all three dogs look up at me dolefully. I go upstairs so that I can look up the mountain, but I can't see Ollie and although I know that Peter Romero is safely in custody I can't help feeling uneasy.

Downstairs again, I turn the old key in the lock and slip down the bolt.

\* \* \*

*Tap, tap, tap.*

I almost jump out of my skin.

The dogs go mad and gallop for the door.

*Tap, tap, tap.*

"Ollie?" I say.

"Yes — it's me," he shouts.

Hauling the dogs back, and opening the door, I see he's with a small woman who looks as if she's been transported from the streets of Milan.

She's talking, "...so you see I can't ring from my mobile and then I saw the lights of the farmhouse and I followed your excellent snowploughed path. I don't know what would have happened if I hadn't."

"Gosh," says Ollie. "What on earth were you doing up here?"

They come through from the hallway. He's taller than her.

"I followed a satnav to Llandovery, and there was a broken-down lorry, so I took a diversion, but..." She shrugs, waving back towards the mountain closing in with darkness. "This wasn't quite what I had in mind. And then my engine cut out and—"

"I'm sure," says Ollie. "We're pretty wild and woolly up here. Lucky you had wellingtons in the car."

"Yes, wasn't it," says the woman.

He waves her past him towards the phone in the kitchen.

I attempt to get the wood burner roaring and Ollie clicks on the sidelights to make the room cosy.

She's very small and neat and doesn't look a bit like someone who would naturally be driving around in Wales. She looks far more like someone from New York or Paris. Apart from the wellies, she's wearing an expensive-looking black padded coat, which she takes off to reveal a neat little red cardigan and some perfectly cut trousers. Huge gold earrings catch the faint golden light coming through the window that faces the mountain. She passes her eyes over me and the house and the dogs.

"Here's the phone," says Ollie, handing her the receiver.

"Oh, thank you," says the woman. She whips off her gloves, snaps open a £700 handbag and retrieves her own phone, clicking through the contacts with perfectly painted long green nails. Diamanté-studded nails. A thought whizzes through my mind and out the other side before I have time to grab it, chased away by her tinkling laugh.

She looks more out of place here than I do.

"You are on your own here?" she asks, casually.

"Yes," says Ollie. "Mum's gone—"

"No," I say, glaring at him. "She's upstairs – she hasn't left yet."

"Oh," says Ollie, raising his eyebrows at me. "Coffee?" he offers with a politeness I've never seen before.

"So kind," the woman looks doubtfully at the overworn kitchen. "Tea, perhaps? Black, weak?"

Ollie nods his head. "Coming up."

She dials. "Oh, hello. Can you help me? I am in a farmhouse, called…?" The woman looks at Ollie.

"It's the Valley Trekking Centre, Valley Farm Stables."

"Yes, and the car is coughing." The woman talks slowly into the phone. "There is something wrong."

She listens.

"Yes,"

I stare at her. I don't care if it's rude.

"Yes, that's right, I am at the farm, right now." She nods. "Yes, there are people here, children – but now would be good, yes, very good. Perfect, see you soon."

She replaces the phone in the cradle and puts her mobile back in her megabucks handbag.

This does not feel right.

"You are brother and sister?" she asks, wandering around the room, peering up the stairs, her eyes moving all the time.

Those sparkly nails.

"No," says Ollie, cheerfully. "She's my cousin."

And something about that hair. "You have a toilet?" she asks.

"Upstairs," says Ollie. "I'll show you."

And the way she's holding her hands.

"No problem," she says, "I'm sure I can find it."

She's even the right height.

"No – I'll just make sure it's decent," he says, running ahead of her.

As I hear their feet on the boards above my head I run to the phone, dial the number the inspector left behind and realise that no one's going to get here in time.

"Hello?" comes the voice on the other end. "DS Parker."

"Maya here," I whisper into the handset. "We need help here, urgently – there's a woman." And then I slam it back and grab the poker from the wood burner.

It was incomprehensible but it should be enough

to get their attention.

The toilet flushes upstairs and I hear a slight scuffle on the landing then Ollie shouts something I can't quite hear.

I get myself ready behind the door that leads upstairs, poker in hand, my mouth completely dry.

It's her.

The woman from the street. I knew I recognised her. Why would she be here if she wasn't part of it?

The poker's shaking. My whole arm's shaking and then I hear the first step.

One

Two

Three

Ollie's head appears.

It's got a gun attached to it, and a hand, and I panic, and I don't drop the poker in time and then they're standing in the room and she's looking at me and I've blown it.

"Maya," she says. "Where is it?"

"What?" I say.

"It," she says.

"What's she talking about?" says Ollie, his head at a really weird angle, a droplet of sweat already pooling on his chin.

"I will shoot him if you don't tell me. The painting, you have it."

"I don't," I say. "How could I have it?"

"You do, I know you do, he told me, yesterday." At that moment, the woman changes the gun from her right hand to her left, the kettle decides to start whistling, Ollie jumps and I bring the poker up hard under her arm, cracking into the gun and watching it arc through the air.

"Got it!" yells Ollie, taking a flying tackle on to the floor and before we even have a chance to go for the woman, she's out the door.

*Bang.*

Ollie fires a shot, taking down a chunk of plaster over the door and the front door crashes closed.

Silence fills the room. The kettle whistles. I dare to breathe.

# Chapter 23

We manage not to shoot Sergeant Lewis when he arrives a few seconds later. He takes the gun, unclips the ammunition and wedges it in his jacket pocket by the door.

"They were sending me back anyway," he says, warming his hands at the wood burner. "Your man's escaped, that's how I got here so quickly."

"Peter Romero?"

"Yup – the car that was taking him to London got into trouble on the ice, tipped up and in the chaos he got away."

"How far away did it crash?" I ask.

"Only about ten miles."

I take a deep breath, and let it out slowly, trying to stop the shuddering that's just started in my chest. "She would have shot you," I say to Ollie.

"Good work with that poker," he says but he's completely white.

"God, sorry I wasn't here," says Sergeant Lewis. "I feel terrible."

"We could just hide in the priest's hole and wait for it all to go away," says Ollie.

"I promised Auntie V we'd feed the horses."

"Of course," says Ollie, with a groan. "We better had. I meant to do it before dark, but she turned up."

The sergeant sighs and rubs his hands together. "Let's get it done now. You stay inside, Maya. Doors locked. Ollie and I will do the horses. We'll knock four times to get in. OK? If you don't hear our knock, don't open the door."

I see them out of the door, dark silhouettes against the midnight blue of the sky. A single snowflake falls from nowhere and settles on my hand before melting. Scanning the mountain over the stable roof I spot nothing. No lights, no people. It's deadly cold out here.

Deadly silent.

I close the door, turning the huge key in the lock, slipping the bolts that Ollie oiled.

The dogs snurfle around my legs and I fill five minutes cutting chunks of disgusting meat out of a can and dropping it into bowls for them. My hands have gone back to the shaking thing.

*Tap, tap, tap, tap.*

I go to the door. "Ollie?"

"It's us, Maya."

The bolts slide open and I turn the key to let them in.

Sergeant Lewis stamps through the door, leaving crusts of boot-shaped snow behind him. "Bloody freezing, out there – and it's starting to snow again. Your ma's not going to get back tonight, I doubt, Ollie."

"You're probably right," he says.

"No matter," says the sergeant. "I'm here – now, shall I rustle up something to eat? I do a very good chickpea curry if I can just find the ingredients. Where's the chopping board? Can I use this one?" He holds up a board.

I know he's being extra cheery, but I just want to be sick.

Ollie sits on the sofa and I sit on the floor. A sofa one side, a wall the other.

"The people or person that kidnapped Zahra was European. She described an accent just like that."

"That woman asked about a picture – do you have it?" asks Ollie.

"No," I don't. "How would I have it? I never actually spoke to him. I was on the bus when…"

I close my eyes. The Vermeer painting was tiny, smaller than a sheet of A4.

"She was holding it," I say. "When I saw them on the street. Holding the painting. There was something in her hand – it looked like a book, but if it's that painting – the Vermeer – it's very small…" I sit back and stare at the ceiling. "But somehow he got it – maybe that's why he ran away?"

"And then he told that woman you had it," says Ollie.

"Why would he do that?"

"Well, do you? Have it?"

"Of course not – but that's why she came here. Not because I was a witness, but because she thinks I have the painting. Which I don't."

"You're sure?" says Ollie. "There's no way you've

got it?"

Sergeant Lewis looks across from the kitchen. "You don't, do you? Not that I've got the faintest idea what you're talking about."

Ollie draws circles in the dust on his computer screen and scrapes off a tiny fly poo with his fingernail. "So how much is this painting worth? If it's the right painting?"

"More than enough to kill for."

\* \* \*

Sitting on the kitchen floor, I ring Inspector Khan. I get DS Parker and tell her my theory.

"She does answer our description of Georgio Romero's girlfriend, but Georgio Romero's girlfriend has a completely cast-iron alibi. She has very reliable witnesses who saw her in Spain around the time of the murder."

"Well I'm pretty sure she's here now, and it was her on Regent Street last week. And she said I have the picture. You've never mentioned a picture."

I hear a sharp intake of breath from the other end of the line.

"*You've* got it?"

"Well no, I haven't, but she thinks I do. She said that he'd told her I did. Which means she's going to come back."

There's a pause.

"I'll get the inspector to call you back just as soon as he can. In the meantime, keep indoors – don't go outside for anything. Keep safe, Maya – I think this could be a major breakthrough."

And the line goes dead.

* * *

We try to be really cheerful and normal through supper. Sergeant Lewis chats away with Ollie, and we eat his delicious curry but it sticks in my mouth.

"Don't worry," he says, seeing me struggle. "No one can get here now. Snow's as thick as my leg."

Auntie V rings. "I'm not even going to try to get home," she says. "It's pelting down and although the foal's been born, I'd like to keep an eye on the mare. Look after the sergeant. There are some chocolate digestives in the cupboard behind the boiler. Have some with a cup of tea."

We don't tell her that we now seem to have *two* homicidal maniacs stalking us.

We drink tea at midnight. Sergeant Lewis decides it's safer if he stays inside the house. I agree.

He and Ollie go out to barricade the gate with some plywood Ollie was saving to make a pool table. "A greater cause, I think," says Sergeant Lewis, brandishing an electric drill. And they return.

"Not even a mouse could get into that yard now," says Sergeant Lewis.

Even so, Ollie closes the shutters on all but the kitchen window.

Together we hammer a board over the inside of the front door.

"Like a castle, this house," says the sergeant, dropping on to the sofa. "Safe as you like."

I notice though that he reunites the gun with its ammunition, and sticks it down the back of his trousers.

I flick through a magazine. We switch on the telly. It's all still about people stuck on motorways and others complaining that someone should have done something about the snow, someone should have known it was coming, someone should be able to magically remove it.

Nothing about Peter Romero escaping, or a woman with long green diamanté nails in the Welsh mountains. Nothing that makes me feel any better.

# Chapter 24

At about one o'clock, I curl up in my room with Megan on the floor. Clutching Zahra's rabbit.

I try to go to sleep. I haven't climbed into my pyjamas because the room is so cold. Dozing is the best I can manage. Sergeant Lewis is staying on guard through the night. The door is bolted and barricaded – I'm safe.

In theory.

I dream, muddled dreams. Of a dragon with huge teeth and a four-by-four that eats ice and lasagne.

And then of a bell ringing in school through the thick snow, and Zahra shouting at me about being a rubbish sister, but the bell keeps going and then I realise that my bum is hanging out the side of the bed and that I can see the wall which is weird because it should be pitch black in here.

BRINNNNNNNNNNNNNNNNNNNNNNN NNNNNNNNNNNG!

I'm awake. My heart thudding. The golden light in my room completely illuminates everything and it's accompanied by roaring, a sound like a thousand waterfalls, and crackling and spitting. "What the…?"

Fire.

I run to the window but I know what I'm going to see.

The stables are silhouetted against the flames. This side, the yard side, isn't burning yet but the far side is orange and yellow and the flames are vivid even through the steam that's coming from the snow. It must be the straw at the back of the stables that's on fire, but in the few moments that I'm watching the flames play along the roof, grabbing at the beams, burning the snow into steam.

And there's a terrible sound of screaming horses.

"Ollie!" I yell, running down through the house, but he's already in the yard.

Here the smell hits me: hot wet singed straw, singed wood. And the heat. The heat is extraordinary. Immediately my head bakes, my hair sticks hotly to my scalp despite the falling snow. A spark lands on my fleece and the little circle of burn races outwards dissolving half the sleeve.

Fleece burns really easily.

"Where's Sergeant Lewis?" I shout.

"I don't know, the bell woke me. Call the fire brigade," shouts Ollie. He struggles with the barn doors, and I rush to help him with the other side. We get the doors open and I see that inside, smoke is already filling the space. Tiny petals of flame flicker across the far side of the building.

The fire brigade can wait. I rush forward to undo the first bolt and let out the first terrified pony. Ollie races down the line, opening the other bolts, so I run for the house. Thundering into the dark kitchen I pick up the phone and try to get a dialling tone. But there isn't one. I click it again, still no sound. I switch on the sidelight so that I can see better, but no lights come on. I bash the receiver against the kitchen top and try again to get a tone. I hold it up to my ear. There's absolutely nothing. No clicks.

In the dark I fumble to find candles but I've no idea where they keep them, so instead I grab my parka, my lovely city parka and hold it under the tap. I drag my fleece off over my head and put the coat over my T-shirt. From the hall I rummage for a woolly bobble hat, again I run it under the tap and jam it on my head. In the porch I find a pair of leather boots which are slightly too big for me. Pouring water over my jeans and wrapping a wet tea towel over my face I go out to face the fire. But the yard is full of horses, plunging and panicking.

They're obviously feeling trapped by the sparks that are gushing into the yard. I rush towards the garden gate, wrenching it open to let the first of the ponies squeeze past me into the thick snow and dark peace of the walled garden behind.

"Go on," I shout to it and chase another through the gap. A third trots towards me, steam rising from its coat and its nostrils flaring and I grab it by the mane and force it into the garden. The others are charging round and round the yard, the dogs barking, all whipping up more panic. But at least they're in the open air.

Looking into the barn, I see that although most

of the looseboxes are open and the ponies have gone, there are three doors still closed at the back. Ollie stands framed against the fire, his arm up against the heat, pushing forwards to the last three doors.

"Ollie! Come out," I shout. "It's no good, it's too dangerous. The roof's going to collapse."

It looks hopeless, the fire has taken hold the length of the building, and it's now burning on three sides. It's only not burning flat out because there probably isn't enough oxygen in there yet, but when the back wall collapses...

Ollie doesn't come out.

Frantically I look around. There are buckets, and a hose rolled up by the front of the house and with fumbling fingers I connect the hose, desperately trying to jam the end on to the tap and turn it on. A freezing jet of water blasts on to the wall in front of me, and I train it on Ollie and the ground immediately in front of him. Wearing my stinking wet coat I advance into the stable aiming the water along the walls, into the hay, into the straw, catching the flickering new flames, but not making much headway with the big ones.

The last loosebox on the right is Samson's.

Ollie's trying to open the bolts on the left. I look up, the ceiling is on fire above us, and the flames have crept right around the sides. The smoke is thick, but my wet tea towel is doing a great job and my wet hat and coat are keeping me cooler. There are two terrified ponies rearing and beating at their doors on Ollie's side. On the right, Samson is still and trembling. I'm still about three metres away, playing the water across the back wall, when one of Ollie's ponies bunches itself up and jumps squarely over the stable door, landing, clattering and skidding in the middle of the barn, and heads unsteadily for the exit.

We should leave with him.

But Ollie's determined to reach the last pony, and so am I.

I soak my coat one more time, and step forward into the flames. The heat's extraordinary, the smell of burning hair surrounds me and I reach out for the bolt on Samson's door. It's too hot so I spray the water on it for a second and try again.

Steam rises from all around me as I struggle to shift it and then, at last, the bolt slides open. I yank the door and step forward into the stable, but the floor sags under my foot and a flaming plank that runs under the door falls away. I step back, and play the water over the flickering straw that surrounds Samson. I need to get him to walk out, but I don't know how to get him through the doorway that is now firmly alight. It's a flaming rectangle and even with my wet coat it feels terrifyingly hot.

Something crashes behind me, and I turn to see that a section of the roof has fallen through.

"C'mon boy," I call to Samson. "C'mon." I leap through the doorway, and get to his side, running my hands through his mane, talking, soothing, trying to keep the fear out of my voice.

Samson stays motionless in the corner of the stable. The flames from the wall tremble and leap across to his tail. I shoot the water over him soaking his coat, forcing him to take a tiny step towards the door.

"Samson it's open, we can walk out!" I shout.

He rolls his eyes at me.

"C'mon, Samson," I say.

Ahead of us, I see Ollie driving the last pony out from the stall, they both run, sparks flying around them, Ollie's coat prickling with feathers of flame. The pony is wearing something over its head.

I'm desperate to run, but I can't leave Samson

and I run the icy water over both of us. I take the tea towel from my face, and try really hard not to breathe more than I have to. I dip it in the water bucket and drape it over Samson's eyes and nose.

On the far side of the barn, a chunk of the roof falls away, showing the whirling snow-filled sky. I clamp my hands under my armpits to stop them shaking.

"Now then, fella," I say, trying to sound like Auntie V. "Let's get out of here."

Samson takes a step forward and stops. We're nearly at the doorway which is completely engulfed in fire. I plunge my hand into my pocket to keep it from the heat and find the bag of liquorice. Under my fingers the pieces feel cool and sticky and I take a handful and hold them out under Samson's nose. His lip curls and he nibbles a single piece.

"Good boy," I say, grabbing a handful of his mane.

I feed him another piece of liquorice and he nuzzles at my pocket.

"Not yet," I say, walking fast towards the doorway.

"One more piece," he grabs it from my fingers.

"This is it, Samson – time to run."

Chucking the last of the bucket over him, I

pull my coat up over my head and charge through the doorway. For an awful moment I can't hear anything but the fire, but then suddenly I hear his hooves on the cobbles and before I'm even halfway through the stable block he charges past, his tail on fire driving him blindly forwards. I rush to follow, and as I make it into the yard, the rending sound of the roof collapsing drowns out everything else. It spews across the gateway cutting us off, leaving us in a wide semicircle of flames.

Samson stops in the yard, turns and shakes the tea towel from his head. Ollie chucks snow at Samson's tail, extinguishing the flames. Chasing him towards the garden and the other horses, I stumble over something large and black in the snow. Samson stops again and skitters, sniffing at the black lump.

"Sergeant Lewis!"

I try to turn him over but he's really heavy. The orange light of the flames flicker across his black uniform and I see that a pool of blood has formed in the snow by his leg.

"Ollie!" I shout.

Ollie staggers towards me, coughing and spluttering. He sees Sergeant Lewis on the ground. "Oh God," he says. "What happened?"

"Get out, get away," mutters the sergeant. "They shot me through the gateway…"

*Crack!*

Ollie and I drop to the ground, splatting into the muddy snow. I realise that the dogs charging back and forth across the yard are probably keeping us safe, making us difficult targets.

"We'll get you to the house," I shout over the roaring sounds coming from the flaming barn.

"Don't bother – get away," he says, but we each grab one of his arms and pull him back into the shelter of the porch.

*Crack!*

"Duck!" yells the sergeant, trying to pull himself into the house and getting as far as possible into the porch.

*Bang!* The sergeant lets off a shot.

*Crack!*

I press my back against the front of the house. I'm out of the line of fire, but I can't stay here forever. Sooner or later someone's going to get through the remains of the stables. And with no phones, we can't call for help.

Across the yard, the sheep are stirring in the crackle from the fire next door, but the old stone roof of their barn seems fireproof despite the cascades of sparks landing from the stables. It looks safe in there. But we'd have to cross the yard.

The stones of the house are warm against my hands. The house feels solid. It wouldn't burn down easily. We could hole up inside, until morning – if we could get inside.

*Crack!*

*Bang!*

The snowman disappears in an explosion of ice.

*Crack!*

The dogs bark louder and the ponies from the garden rush out into the yard, and charge round, neighing and stamping and thundering and stopping dead. Terrified.

They're not the only ones.

Next to me, Ollie crouches behind the water butt.

*Pfft!* A bullet bounces in the mud right in front of us and skips off into the blackness.

They're getting closer.

*Crack!*

"We can't stay here," says Ollie. "I'm going to make a break for the house."

"Don't," I shout.

*Zing!*

Bullets fly from the other direction.

"Ah!" A cry comes from the gateway, and someone fires again from the garden.

*Zing!*

*Zing!*

"What?" says Ollie. "Is someone there?" he shouts.

Samson whinnies and gallops past us, followed by another horse and they head straight for the sheep barn. I can't see well enough, but I think one of them leaps over the hurdles while the other skids to the side at the last second.

The dogs bark and jump and yelp. *Zing!*

*Crack!*

*Zing!*

We're trapped between the fire from both sides.

"Who is it?" Ollie shouts towards the garden. "Who's there?"

*Zing!*

*Crack!*

"Keep down!" someone shouts.

*What?*

Pieces of the jigsaw tumble into place. The way he followed me, the fact he didn't shoot us when he came to the farm. The woman. The picture.

"Peter Romero," I shout.

"Yes!" comes the answer.

*Zing!*

"How'd you get in?" Ollie yells towards the garden.

"Over the garden wall," the voice returns.

*Crack!*

*Zing!*

I feel safer. And then I don't.

*Zing!*

*Crack!*

We're still stuck against a farmhouse in a hail of bullets. Just because someone's firing in the opposite direction, it doesn't make it any less likely we'll die.

*Crack!*

*Crack!*

*Zing!*

"Is there a way out of the yard?" I say to Ollie.

"I've been thinking," he says. "There's a pile of straw blocking the back exit in the sheep barn – we might get through. We could take the Land Rover," he says. "Except the tank is empty."

"We'll take ponies if we can."

Bullets fly again and a figure hurtles out of the darkness, flattening itself against the wall next to me.

"Pleased to meet you. Peter Romero at your service. Glad you're still alive, Maya," he says. "Can either of you fire a gun?"

"Don't ask them to," calls Sergeant Lewis. "But I could do with another one, this is just a toy," he says, his voice faint. "Ty Fawr rifle club champion – 1977," Peter Romero hands a rifle around the corner of the porch, and the sergeant lets off a round.

*Bang!*

It's so loud my eyes water. "Let's get out of here," I say, but standing completely still, feeling the comforting warmth of Peter Romero at my side, and wondering if I've got the courage to leave it.

"Good idea. Go," he says. "We'll hold them here as long as we can."

*Crack!*
*Zing!*
*Bang!*
*Crack!*

"Ready, cuz?" shouts Ollie, pulling his coat up around his ears and pushing off from the side of the house. He charges through the yard, running straight for the sheep barn. Eight paces and he's over the hurdles at the front.

*Crack!*

*Bang!*

*Crack!*

*Bang!*

"Come on, Maya!"

*Zing!*

*Crack!*

*Bang!*

I say goodbye to my family, blow them an imaginary and pointless kiss, and run, my head down, my body wired so that in ten paces I'm by the barn and springing over the hurdle is easy.

*Zing!*

*Zing!*

*Zing!*

I pile into Ollie, he's crouched on the other side.

"I don't think they even saw you," he says.

"Where's the gap we can get through?" I say, peering into the darkness, trying to keep the shake out of my voice.

"Here." We wade through the sheep, the smell of singed wood from the burning stable next door, strong, but not overwhelming. The sheep shuffle and baa, hiding our movement. A white pony looms out of the darkness. Ollie grabs it and leads us both to a tower of straw bales. Together we shift enough to make a doorway.

"But we need two ponies," I say. "We won't make it on one."

Ollie puts his fingers in his mouth and lets out a really loud whistle. In the yard, a pony pauses and gallops towards the sheep barn, easily clearing the hurdles and clattering into the sheep.

"Wow!" I say, grabbing his mane. "Samson?"

# Chapter 25

Trying not to panic, we take badly fitting tack from the Land Rover parked behind the stables, we mount up and a few minutes later I realise that we're on the track up the mountain. Even from up here I can smell the smouldering wood despite the snow circling around us, muffling everything. A lone dog trots out behind us and falls in with the horses.

"Megan, go back," says Ollie.

But the dog ignores him and trots alongside.

I glance back. I can't really see much except for the glow of the embers, although there's a greyness to the sky that probably signals dawn.

More gunfire echoes below and Samson quivers with each shot. Peering through the circling snow, guns flash, both sides of the yard. A second later, the sound of the shots reaches us. Like lightning and thunder.

"S'all right, boy," I mutter, heading Samson up the track, and he breaks into a desperate attempt to trot.

"How long before they work out where we've gone?" Ollie shouts.

"I don't know," I say. "It depends on Sergeant Lewis, and Peter Romero."

"The gunman who isn't the gunman, you mean?"

"Yes – the one who is currently shooting everyone on our behalf," I say, almost making myself smile. "Do we stand any chance of getting over the mountain? Or should we try to go through to the main road?"

"The mountain's our best bet – although we're going to have to be very careful that we don't ride straight over the cliff at the side."

Despite the bulldozing yesterday, the snow's fallen so heavily that the tracks have gone – it's more like the depression in a mattress than a path and I remember the steep drop that lies to our left. I wonder if Samson would sense it.

The snow whips against my cheeks, very quickly removing the last scraps of heat from the fire and I pull my collar up. I've only got a T-shirt on under this coat and the wind's cruel. Samson's black fur is turning white and I realise that we may soon become almost invisible. Ollie's pony is invisible.

Megan's invisible.

Good.

We press on up through the snow, the ponies' hooves almost silent, but each step is accompanied by a slight crunching.

Samson stops quite suddenly, his ears swivelling, listening. I listen too. Behind us, there's shouting – and an engine revving. He grunts and strides out, following Ollie, as if he perfectly understands what's going on and I lean forward along his neck hoping the thickening snow will bounce from my back rather than collecting on my hands and face. We walk on up the track and I look back to see how clear our tracks are.

Too clear.

Samson picks his way up the path – I imagine he knows it as well as Ollie – and we're quickly by

Ollie's side.

"They'll be with us soon," says Ollie. "What do we do?"

"We ride to the quarry," I say. "Make a stand."

The words sound ridiculously brave, ridiculously certain and I wonder if I'm determined enough to make this work.

"OK," Ollie shouts. And he urges his pony on up the hill.

I let Ollie go on and hold Samson back for a moment, turning in the saddle to look back down the hillside.

The flashes are still lighting up the yard. Four from one side, two from the other. Then headlights play through the snow, two vehicles. Four-by-fours? They wouldn't have reached the farm if they weren't. They're bouncing up and down, making heavy weather of the ground. Behind them are two sets of smaller lights. Also bouncing, but moving fast, like spiders. Snowcats? Quad bikes?

Samson pauses, moving his feet, anxious. He's not the only one. But if we can hold it together, he can help me. He probably knows more than I do about escape.

I look up ahead. There's no way of knowing how

much further the quarry is. I know that if I keep the wall on my right, then the huge drop should be easy to avoid.

I wonder if our pursuers know that.

I flex my frozen fingers around Samson's reins.

"Come on Samson," I murmur. "Time to get going."

* * *

I squeeze his sides and point him up the hill. He lurches forwards until we catch up with Ollie. Samson doesn't try to bite anyone, and I wonder if he's too cold to try.

"The little trucks, we need to use them," I shout into the wind. "Do they run? Will they work through this snow?"

"On the rails you mean?"

"Yes."

"Maybe," he says. "Maybe, I don't remember them ever working."

We plug on up, the horses with shelves of snow collecting on their rumps.

"Good boy, Samson," I say meaninglessly, and a load of snowflakes settle on my tongue. I can't hear anything, only the wind, which cuts icily around my throat and wrists. My feet have long since frozen solid but Samson keeps plodding on and I keep my eye on the wall to the right, horribly aware of the huge drop to the left. I can't see it, everything more than a metre away is just white and then I begin to see the top of the mountain, a grey mass ahead of me that must be the quarry.

Samson sees it too and attempts a trot which quickly turns back into a walk.

Stepping into the mine is like entering another world. The awful wind drops and although it's still snowing it's calm and beautiful in here.

I ride right into the mine, slip down from Samson's back and try to hook the reins over a bracket. They hang loose. I don't seem to have the co-ordination.

Samson carefully removes the reins from the ground and holds them between his teeth. He follows me as I walk to the trucks, standing a little way away and watching me.

Ollie leaps down to join me. All the trucks are snow-covered, but they're also all filled with slate, as if about to leave for their final journey.

"What are we doing here?" he asks, his voice sounding as panicky as I feel. "They'll find us really soon. We could just go straight through and down the other side."

"I know," I say, pushing at the first truck. "But they'll catch us up on the way down, they've got quad bikes or something – we have to slow them down, we have to get them out of their vehicles." The words are really hard to form, my jaw seems to have frozen. My tongue feels huge and useless in my mouth. "Give me a hand Ollie."

I put my frozen hands on the truck and push.

The truck groans but stays put.

"What are you doing?"

"If we can set it rolling, we can send it down the mountain. All we need to do is get them to veer over the cliff."

Ollie puts his shoulder on the other corner and pushes. The truck grinds forward but doesn't rush to run away down the mountain.

"Oil!" he shouts and darts behind the bulldozer to get an oilcan. Something that looks like orange sorbet globs out and smears over the rusty wheels of the truck.

I rock the truck back towards me, and Ollie pushes it forward.

"Try again," he shouts and I turn my back, pushing alongside him with my bum.

Digging my heels into the track I shove as hard as I can. The truck begins to roll freely and we turn, giving it the slightest shove with our hands, and by the time we leave the edge of the mine, it's heading downhill at speed all on its own.

We watch it tip into the blizzard, rolling away in silence. There's no sound, no crash or bang or anything.

"Again?" I say.

We take another truck and oil the wheels and then shove, and shove, and the second truck picks up speed and plummets into the blizzard.

This time there's a crash and the sound of slate skidding over metal. Someone below us shouts and through a whorl in the snow, I see headlights sweep right across the mountain. Behind me, Samson shudders a little but stays close by.

"Again," shouts Ollie.

The third truck's harder to move, but we get it rolling and it shoots off. We definitely get a yell this time, with more metal sounds, and breaking glass and someone shouting in a language I don't recognise.

Ollie lines up the last truck. "We could just send this one down and then run."

"I think we should hang on to that one," I say. "Just in case. How do we get out?"

"That gate, there." He points to the back of the quarry.

"Where would we get to?"

"Down the other side you sort of find the village, but it's not easy – certainly not in this."

"Could they drive it?"

Ollie nods. "On quad bikes, I'd think so."

I look towards the gate and I realise that it's almost light. Everything's colourless, but everything's visible.

That includes us.

*Crack!*

"Duck," I shout.

"What the…?" Ollie steps forward leaving the cover of the truck.

A puff of snow bounces into the air at the back of the quarry. Samson whinnies.

A third shot sounds, this time pinging off the last little truck.

"Bloody hell!" shouts Ollie, throwing himself down.

*Crack!*

A fourth bounces off the bulldozer cab. Megan

yelps and runs for the back of the quarry.

"We need to get out of here and we need to get to the bulldozer to block the entrance," I shout. "Have you got the key?"

"Totally," says Ollie, crawling across the quarry floor.

*Crack!*

Another bullet races towards us and dings on the bulldozer blade.

Samson resists as I pull him towards the gate at the back, but the other pony can't wait to get out so together they cram through the gap.

"Now stay here," I say, hopefully, looping their reins over the gatepost.

Headlights swing into the quarry, lighting up the distance between me and the bulldozer. A four-by-four growls at the entrance.

*Crack!*

*Zing!*

Flashes light up the cab of the four-by-four and I realise Peter Romero has made it to the top of the mountain in the Land Rover. He's there, firing down the hill. Protecting us.

But we've got our own plans.

A bullet ricochets off the cage on top of the

bulldozer cab and pings into the snow in front of me.

"Now, Ollie!" I shout.

I reach down to find a piece of snowy slate.

*Crack!*

"Peter Romero's in your truck on the left," I shout, banging the fuel pump so hard the slate shatters in my hand.

And we start her up.

# Chapter 26

In spite of the snow, the noise in the quarry is immense. I can't speak to Ollie, I can only watch as he heads towards the edge of the quarry and into the blizzard. Bullets ping off the blade of the bulldozer, and past, hitting the slate and sending small avalanches around my head and ears.

I duck, tuck my arms under my armpits and head for the back of the mine. Samson stands there, his eyes white and rolling, his whole body trembling with fear as I race towards the gate. He snaps and pulls back against his reins. The other horse looks ready to run too. I stand with them, trying to say calming things, wondering if I've spoken to Ollie for the last time, wondering how I'll explain his death to Auntie V.

"Maya!" shouts Ollie, hurtling towards me.

"But the bulldozer!" I say. "It's still going?"

"I jammed the pedal down."

I swing into Samson's saddle, trapping fresh snow between him and my bum. "That means the entrance won't be blocked."

"No – but it'll take them longer to recover from the bulldozer than to clamber round it." He jumps on to his pony. "Listen."

He's right – I can hear the truck revving and someone screaming and the bulldozer roaring. All the gunshots stop.

Beneath me, Samson trembles. His breathing is heavy and panicked, but he seems to recover quite quickly once I wrap my frozen hands around the stiffening reins.

Ollie points, and I see a faint dip in the snow.

"If we can find it, there's a path," he says. "It's about three miles down the mountain to the village."

"You go ahead," I say. "You know the way."

He shuffles into the snow. The blizzard closes in around him, and I feel horrible watching him vanish, as if I might never see him again. I glance back into the quarry. The headlights are shining towards me now, but the bulldozer grinds forward, towards the other headlights, and there's a terrible sound of metal on metal. The lights move from horizontal to vertical, rising into the sky, the snow slanting straight down the yellow beams towards a strange dark rearing shape, which as the bulldozer engine roars, tumbles away down the mountain, out of sight.

The bulldozer revs again and there are gunshots and I think I hear someone cry out.

"C'mon, Maya," shouts Ollie. I look down towards him. They're just visible.

"Ok, Samson, take it steady," I say and gently squeeze his sides.

Samson's head jerks up and he shivers as he follows the grey shape disappearing down the mountain. Ollie's trail is clear, the snow has fallen less on this side than the other, and in places the wind has blown the snow to almost nothing, but I'm aware that to me, the path is completely unfamiliar. It may not be for Ollie and Samson though. The break in the snow is short because within seconds, the snowstorm closes around us and the gunshots up the hill become muffled. I almost stop worrying about them and find myself concentrating on Samson's uneven breathing, his hooves skidding from time to time on stones and on not losing sight of Ollie.

The white is blinding now that dawn's breaking through. I almost can't see and I wonder how Samson is negotiating it. It's as if he's decided to take me with him. He could just dump me and gallop on down the mountain, but in some curious way he seems to be taking care of me.

This human that can't ride. One that doesn't know anything about the mountain.

For what must be half an hour we head steadily downwards.

Gradually he slows, and I realise that I've lost sight of Ollie.

"Ollie!" I shout into the wind.

"Ollie!" but he can't hear me.

"C'mon Samson," I say, "look sharp."

But he's almost strolling now. As if he's asleep.

I slip down from his back, take the reins over his head and walk alongside him, talking, chattering, encouraging.

The hillside flattens out so we stumble more

easily, a little faster, still in Ollie's tracks.

"We're getting there, almost down, nearly there and I expect there's a nice warm stable, with hay and water and..."

Water?

I realise that Samson probably hasn't had any water since the fire. He must be exhausted. He's probably suffering from smoke inhalation too. Isn't that what people die of in fires?

I stop for a minute to look at him. There's a glimmer of daylight now, not enough to show colours properly but enough to see him. He's in a sorry state with tufts of burned mane and tail and his thick coat singed in places.

And I asked him to carry me up a mountain, into a gunfight and then down the other side. And he didn't run and he didn't throw me off.

I look around for grass or water. A trough? A spring? But everything's just white. White up, white down, white forwards – so much white.

His lips nuzzle around my hand and collar. Perhaps he remembers the liquorice. "I've got nothing," I say, and then remember the sheep digging through the snow to reach the grass.

Looking up, the sky is darkening again and the

blizzard thickens with the day. I'm in a silent snow-filled world of my own with an exhausted pony and I'm beginning to wonder which way is down. I scrape away the snow, pull up a tiny shred of yellowy green grass and wave it under Samson's nose. I'm surprised but gratified to find that he can eat with the bit in his mouth. He tries the end, and perks up as he nibbles the grass delicately, running his lips over it before embedding his teeth. He nuzzles his head into the hole I've made and tugs a few more strands out as I pull more snow away.

After a minute or two, he shakes his head and blows through his nostrils showing signs of waking up. I grab a handful of the lightest freshest snow and hold it under his mouth. He licks a little so I try again.

We walk alongside each other through the snow, dropping slowly down the hillside, meandering in and out of the other pony's fading hoofprints. A little further on, and Samson stumbles, almost falling to the ground.

Another fifty metres and he stumbles again, this time falling to his knees before standing.

We stop. I can hear the snow falling. I can hear it rustling as it settles on Samson's back. He tilts his back leg and drops his head as if he's going to sleep.

"Now look, Samson. You're going to have to come with me. I can't leave you here," I say.

He blasts little fragments of grass through his nose in a snotty sneeze and jerks his head up.

"OK," I say. "Come on, let's get down this hill."

Slowly, I step out along the path left by Ollie's pony.

Samson walks behind me, placing his feet carefully in the other pony's footprints.

"Ollie?" I call.

"Ollie?"

A brown shape bounds through the snow.

"Megan," I say. "Am I glad to see you!"

She barely stops to greet me before turning and heading back into the snow and I follow, almost sure of keeping her in sight. It must mean that Ollie isn't far away, and I try to get Samson to speed up, but he's slow.

Maybe he's being careful.

We plod on.

It's eerily quiet now. I can't hear anything. Or almost nothing. No gunshots, but something above me is making a sound. Someone's walking through the snow, they're stumbling on the stones and tussocks but they're moving quite fast.

It could be Peter Romero, but it might not be.

Samson's ears twirl. He's listening too.

"Hurry up, fella," I whisper. "I think we may have company."

Samson obliges, picking up speed and I stumble along next to him. Down the mountain, the snow's like white soup, blocking out everything and I'm becoming increasingly aware that Megan's disappeared again, and that the hoofprints we've been following are becoming almost impossible to spot.

It's hard to hear over our own snow squeaking, but I think someone behind us is definitely making more progress than we are. I pull Samson on and he almost trots. I think he can hear our pursuer and he's probably remembered the gunshots up at the quarry.

"Steady on," I whisper, but Samson's going for it now, so I try an authoritative tug on his reins.

"Stop." He almost does. I jam my foot in the stirrup and start to slither on to the snow-covered saddle as he picks up speed down the hill.

He drops and rises and staggers but keeps going,

he rather than me, following a path. Carrying us down, carrying us further and further away from whoever is chasing us.

"Good, boy," I mutter, more to reassure myself than Samson, and turn round to see if I can see our pursuer. I can't, but they could be twenty metres behind, because twenty metres behind is a wall of blizzard.

I lean forwards on to Samson's neck and try really hard to trust him. He seems sure – far surer than me but I don't like this at all. He was exhausted earlier and I'm really aware that he must be desperate for proper food and water.

It feels like ages, stumbling down that hillside, completely blind, completely silent but leaving a deadly set of prints in the snow for anyone to follow. I may even have dozed off.

Suddenly, there's water.

A stream, burbling through the snow, sweeping fast down the hill. And cutting us off.

I look for prints, horse or dog, but I can't see any. Stupid me, I wasn't looking and I don't know where Megan went. I daren't risk calling, so I slip down from Samson's back and test the depth of the water. It comes up to the top of my boots, Samson plunges his nose into the stream and drinks.

I really hope it doesn't hurt a horse, drinking ice-cold water. I vaguely remember it being bad for people but I haven't the heart to yank his head up and so I join him, sucking up mouthfuls of the stuff, realising how thirsty I am.

I listen out for the person following us, but the stream cuts out all other sound.

Our footprints are clear on the bank though.

"We're going to have to go through it," I whisper, mostly to myself. "And I'll have to ride you."

I pull myself up into the saddle and Samson obligingly wades into the water. All the stories I've ever heard of people being swept downstream by flood waters rush to my mind. The rivers always look so innocent when the TV people go to film them after a tragedy but this stream doesn't look a bit innocent. It looks deep and icy and black.

Samson staggers downstream before skidding, and then lunging at the other side, which is too steep, so we have to pick our way further down until the far bank is lower. He hesitates for a second, trembling, then springs up, scrabbling at the snow, his hooves skittering all over the sides. I lean forward to help him get out of the water, reaching out to the bank with my hands.

"C'mon, boy, you can do it."

We're making a racket, there's no way we could go unseen after this.

*Crack!*

I hear the sound and then realise that the little jump of snow that came to my right must have been a bullet.

Samson hears it too and bunches for a giant effort, leaping out of the water; his hooves thrash at the snow, catching and just making the bank. He stands quivering on the side, steam rising from his coat, snow falling on his head.

He stops for a second before breaking into a tentative trot as we head out into the blizzard, blind, clueless and under fire.

*Crack!*

Another bullet. A little to the left this time, and Samson lumbers into an awkward run, breathing hard and even from up here showing the whites of his eyes.

'S'all right, lad,' I say, although I don't believe it myself. 'We'll be all right.'

*Crack!*

And he falls beneath me.

"No!" I shout, tumbling to the ground with him. He tries to get up but I can see that he's been hit, his foreleg grazed, ribbons of blood spilling across the snow.

"Samson, no!" I say again as if I can tell him to stop bleeding. All I have left are my gloves. I take them off and hold them against the wound. The blood bubbles up around the side and then seems to slow.

"Good boy, brave boy," I say. I sound like my mum when the twins have fallen over.

*Crack!*

A bullet whizzes over my head.

Samson kicks with his back legs, desperate to get on his feet.

"Up you get," I say, panic rising in my throat. "Come on! You can do it. You're the toughest horse on the mountain. The meanest pony in the stables, come on, come on."

*Crack!*

Another bullet whisks past my cheek.

Samson thrashes and with my help, stands, juddering with pain and fear.

"Good boy," I say, trying to sound really calm. "Let's walk a little, eh?"

*Crack!*

He jerks forwards, his head nodding with every pace, the whites of his eyes showing. Blood spatters red ink blots on to the snow before sinking into the whiteness.

One step

Two

Three

Four

"Brilliant," I say.

*Crack!*

An explosion of snow immediately in front of Samson makes him rear, stagger and fall again. This time, sinking deep into a drift, as if he realises it's no good.

I lie, almost flat on the ground and stroke his nose.

"Come on you brave little horse. Up you get." I pull at the rein, but his head's heavy and he won't lift it. Snow settles on his black eyelashes, and he sinks into the whiteness.

The blood melts the snow around his leg and no matter how hard I press, I can't stop it. There's so much. And it's so red against the white.

Raising his head one last time, he tries to reach

his leg with his nose, but he can't, he falls back against the snow, and then, when the next snowflake falls on his eye, he doesn't even blink.

The blood seems to slow.

The snow stops melting.

He doesn't seem to breathe.

"Samson?"

"Samson?"

But he doesn't move. He doesn't move at all.

# Chapter 27

Blinded by tears, I run, headlong down the mountain and then, just as I'm feeling that I might be heading for a cliff, a low brown shape races across the snow towards me.

"Megan," I say, and she bounces against me, before tearing off ahead towards a black building looming from the blizzard. I run for it. It turns out to be a barn, but a barn with a track that's been cleared at some point in the last twenty-four hours.

I catch up with her, and grabbing a skanky length of twine sticking out through the snow, loop it around her collar like a lead.

I don't want to lose her too.

In the shelter of the building I get my breath back and for a moment I consider hiding inside. I'd be out of the wind, in the almost warmth, but then I imagine myself trapped with the gunmen outside. Megan obviously thinks it's a bad idea, she growls and pulls me back towards the track. I suspect it goes in the direction of the village that I know must be down here somewhere. The ground rises and we cross the river on an open-sided concrete bridge, still running although Megan seems inexhaustible while my lungs are screaming and my legs are screaming louder.

Another building appears on my right – another barn and we keep up the pace until I see a house with a light on, and a road and more houses.

Thank God. The village.

The houses are clustered together surrounded by stone walls. Everything looks pretty picture-perfect but I need to get somewhere secure, fast. In the middle of the village is a street light, a couple of cars covered in thick snow and a distant unlit petrol station.

I stop, reaching for breath and try to think what to do, but all I can think about is Samson's body going cold in the snow.

It must be about eight o'clock, surely people are up by now, ready to go to work.

I look for a shop but there doesn't seem to be one. Instead I pick the house with the most welcoming front door, a Christmas wreath and a light on upstairs.

The green door doesn't seem to have a bell or a knocker so I hammer with my fist.

"Hold on, hold on," comes a voice from inside, and a woman in a dressing gown opens the door. Behind her, a boy.

"Gethin!" I say, hugely relieved. "Help me. Samson's been shot and Sergeant Lewis is back at the farm – he's hurt too, and I've no idea where Ollie is."

"Goodness," says Gethin's mum. "Look at the state of you – come on in child,"

"Maya?" Gethin says. "Is that you? What's happened? Oh, Megan too."

*Crack!*

Next to me the door frame explodes in a fountain of chippings.

"Good Lord!" says Gethin's mum and she drags me in, slamming the door and sliding a huge bar down behind it. "What's going on?"

"There's no—" I start.

Glass crashes in the room next door.

"Oh my word!" she says, reaching for the telephone. She runs for the giant fireplace and stands inside the inglenook prodding at the phone.

*Crack!*

A bullet races through the broken window and stops in the wall opposite. We all dive on the floor.

"Look I don't want to put you in danger – I need to get out of here," I shout.

"Take the truck," says Gethin's mum, the phone against her ear. "Police, please," she says.

"C'mon," says Gethin, rising to crouch and scuttling through to the back of the house and out into the yard. There's a truck standing there and he signals that I should climb into the passenger seat. I clamber up and he leaps into the driving seat.

"Can you drive?" I ask.

"Of course," he says, "I'm a farmer's son." He guns the engine and we grind across the yard, hurtling out through the gate, past two figures in snowsuits.

The back window of the truck shatters.

"Bloody hell!" shouts Gethin, gunning the engine

even more, and swaying from side to side.

"Can we get out of the village?"

"No – the internal roads are open but there was a small avalanche between here and the main road." We skid through a pile of snow. "We need a tractor to clear it but Dad's dealing with the cows. I'm sorry but we're trapped for now. I'm trying to think where to take you."

"Do you know if there's a police station, and if it has a cell?"

"There's definitely a police station. There'll be no one there, though, but they always leave it open. Why?"

I check my pockets. I've still got my phone, and it's still got battery.

"I've an idea," I say, wondering if I've gone completely mad.

* * *

Gethin dumps me by the police station.

"Take care," he says. "I think you should just lock yourself inside – but…"

"I've got a chance to do this right – I'm going to take it," I say. "Just find Ollie."

The truck skids a little and Gethin shoots off up the lane towards the mountain.

I hammer on the door before realising that it's open just as Gethin said.

"Hello?" I call.

It's a tiny place. An office with a telephone on a desk, not even a computer, a huge coat rack hung with all sorts of police coats and hats, and at the back a heavy black door with a small slidey hatch in it. A real prison cell. The keys of the cell are hanging in the outside of the door. Inside is a bed, an empty bucket and a pile of blankets. Also a whole stack of paperwork that's probably been waiting to go somewhere for years.

I reckon I've got about twenty minutes before they catch up with me. I load the paperwork on the bed and cover it with the blankets, then I get my phone and record myself talking, with gaps as if I was making a call.

It lets me record for fifteen minutes before it cuts out. I hope that's long enough.

I press play, and lay the phone into the bucket. The bucket amplifies the sound and together with the old brick walls of the cell it all sounds like I'm in there – talking to someone. Opening the door, a crack, I close the slidey hatch, and leave the keys hanging in the outside of the lock.

Next I take a snow shovel from the wall by the desk, yank a load of coats off the rack, put them just outside the cell next to the door, and burrow inside them.

I don't need to open the outside door – my footprints through the thick snow lead straight in. And the village is so small, it won't take them long to find me.

I wait.

\* \* \*

My recording must be reaching an end when I hear running footsteps. There are no shouts. So I don't think it's Gethin or Ollie – the feet sound too big. I stay mouse-still. For an age there's someone outside.

I sit under my coats inside, listening. Something creaks, and there's stamping in the doorway.

My recording goes quiet. It's run out. I only hope they heard it.

Someone whispers.

"Shhh," says another voice.

The door opens really slowly. I can just see it through a gap in the coats. The woman stands, looking around the tiny police station with a huge man I've never seen right behind her. I hold my breath.

They listen. My phone beeps.

It seems to take forever, but then they rush forward, both of them into the cell and I take my chance, shoving the door shut with my snow shovel. Someone screams and pushes against it, but the door's heavy and I've got the advantage of surprise – and some big bolts.

"Hey!" shouts the woman as I turn the key.

*Bang!*

The sound of a gun going off inside the small space is massive. Deafening. But the old door holds. And there are no holes in it.

Or me.

And then I sit on the floor, my back buried in the police coats, and shake.

# Chapter 28

About an hour later, when I've rung the police from the police phone and they've got confused before they've understood and told me that all available forces are at the farm dealing with the aftermath of a gun battle but they will send someone as soon as possible, Helen the policewoman turns up on foot.

Gethin's with her – they've been searching for Ollie.

"You mean he hasn't come down from the mountain yet?" I think of the gunshots. "Oh, no!"

"Don't worry," Helen says. "Ollie knows that

hillside like the back of his hand."

"And there's no better horseman in the valleys," adds Gethin.

"And there's Samson," I say.

"Who the ruddy hell's Samson?" asks Helen, suddenly looking completely exhausted.

"The horse I came down on. They –" I point at the cell – "shot him. I had to leave him…" My voice trembles. Now I've said it out loud I've got this awful picture in my head of Samson bleeding away into the snow all alone.

"Do you think he's still alive?" asks Gethin.

"I don't know," I say, trying and failing to hold back the tears.

Gethin looks embarrassed and Helen hands me a police-tissue.

"Right, I can't deal with wounded horses right now – I'm sure he'll be fine," says Helen, taking her walkie-talkie from her belt. "And what about whoever you've got in there – armed is it?"

"Yes," I say, sniffing hard. "But the door's holding really well."

"It would," says Helen. "My pa made it. But it's going to be a heck of a job getting them out. And I'm not paid enough to try."

*** 

A little later, when Helen's made about a thousand phone calls and fed me the police supply of emergency chocolate hobnobs, Gethin's dad arrives on a tractor with Auntie V following behind on the quad bike. He announces that the village is reconnected to the main road.

But he hasn't seen Ollie.

"What?" says Auntie V. She looks as exhausted as I feel. Blackened, sooty, wet and white-faced. "You mean my son's up there on the mountain in a blizzard?" She leans on the tractor and I watch tears race down her face. And then she reaches her arms out to me and holds me tight in the strongest hug.

"Have you seen the stables?" I say.

She nods, her mouth wobbling.

"We got them all out. Ollie did."

She nods again.

"Ollie's very determined," I say, mumbling it into her chest.

"I know, love, like you," she says, her voice all high and unsteady. "He's a chip off the old block."

"He'll make it safely down," I say. Wishing I believed it.

"I'm sure," she lies. "I'm sure."

* * *

The mountain-rescue people arrive in four-by-fours to look for Ollie. They're dressed in orange, scarily official. They talk about body bags and stretchers and I get images of Ollie dangling from a helicopter all broken.

"Don't think about it," says Gethin.

Auntie V sits in a car with the mountain-rescue coordinator. I sit there with her, but I can't relax, I feel terrible about Samson.

"Go and look for him, then," she says. "I want to stay here, but I'm sure Gethin will go with you."

Leaving her white-faced and tearful in the car feels bad, but the vision of Samson bleeding in the snow won't go away. I promise we'll be as quick as we can, and Gethin's dad says he'll help.

We take an enormous blue tractor and trailer and all cram into the cab, something which at any other time would be really exciting. I tell them I came over a concrete bridge with no sides and past a barn and Gethin's dad seems to know exactly where it is.

"So what did the place look like? Where you left the pony?"

I try to describe the stream, with the steep banks, and then big flat bits that I ran across and I realise that trying to find Samson is going to be like trying to find a needle in a haystack.

"Lucky he's a black horse, really," jokes Gethin's dad. But nobody laughs.

The snow's still falling, but it's lighter now, and I get a glimpse up towards a hedge.

I don't know why, but somehow it feels right and I point. "That way, I think."

Gethin's dad stops the tractor and we pile out, searching.

"How much snow will have fallen since he was shot – I wonder?" says Gethin, asking the question that's been running through my mind.

"He'll shake it off," I say, "and if I stopped the bleeding, then..." My voice catches.

We walk up to the stream and Gethin finds the place where Samson and I struggled out.

"Hoofprints!" yells Gethin's dad, and then a second later. "I found him – bloody hell! He's alive!"

I stumble over the snow, running towards Gethin and his dad who are brushing at something. There he is. There's Samson, still lying down, but very much alive having cleared a circle of snow and nibbling at the winter grass beneath. His coat is covered in a light sprinkling of snow, but still a long way from becoming an iceberg.

"Samson! Samson!" I yell and rush over to hug his black furry neck.

He snorts, shakes his head, and bites me full on the leg.

\* \* \*

It takes an age to persuade Samson into the trailer, but Gethin and his dad seem to know exactly how to do it, and when we get him back into their village, it feels like a huge victory.

As we're going into Gethin's house, a helicopter arrives. It brings Inspector Khan and some police negotiators who will be able to get the woman and her accomplice out of the cell. But it flies away again because apparently it's the wrong sort of helicopter for mountain rescue.

"But I want it to look for Ollie," I say to the inspector when he comes in.

"There are plenty of people out there already looking on the ground."

"Well, I want to join them."

"No," says Inspector Khan, searching the room

for somewhere safe to sit. Somewhere free of food, animals, children and glass. "I need your statement – you're tired, you're in shock. It's possible you've captured two members of a gang that Interpol have been looking at for years. I think you can drink hot chocolate and eat biscuits for now."

"Don't patronise me!" I snap, and for the first time since I met Inspector Khan, he laughs. Not in a bad way.

Auntie V comes back into the room and slumps into a chair.

"We found Samson," I say. "He's fine."

Megan sits on the floor and puts her heavy head on Auntie V's knee. Absently, Auntie V ruffles the dog's brown ears. "Good," she says, "that's good." But I can see it's not what she's been hoping to hear.

Gethin's mum is busy trying to keep two little kids out of the way, and failing. They remind me of Ishan and Precious. They're little and ordinary and funny and I want to go home. I suddenly really want to go home.

"Can I ring home?" I ask Gethin's mum.

"Of course," she says, handing me the phone.

I get Granddad and give him a garbled version

of the story – which probably sounds worse than it is. After all, the gunmen are safely locked away so Ollie's only up against the blizzard now.

"Is your Auntie V all right?" he asks.

I glance over to where Auntie V's sitting on the sofa, staring into a cup of tea, tears rolling through the soot on her face.

"I hope so – it's awful, Granddad – the stables are completely destroyed, it's her whole life."

"And Ollie?" says Granddad.

"Yes – and Ollie."

"But it's not your fault, love," says Granddad, quickly. "Not your fault at all. You tried to do the right thing."

"Yes," I say.

Granddad's voice goes all gravelly. "I'll have a word with her – if she's up to it."

I take the phone to Auntie V and go to the bathroom to wash my face.

* * *

We eat cheese sandwiches. Inspector Khan picks balls of cheese from his plate with the pad of his finger.

"What about Peter Romero?" I ask him. "Is he all right? I think he came to the top of the mountain.

He was trying to keep them back."

"Sergeant Lewis is in hospital – I didn't know about Romero." He heads off into a corner and starts typing things into his phone.

A snowplough arrives. And several teams of police people in more white suits to pick over the crime, the fire, the quarry.

Auntie V stands at the window and looks worried. They won't let her look for Ollie either. "But it's mad – I know the mountain so well – I've got the best chance of finding him."

Gethin goes to search. And Helen, and most of the village.

Policemen and people in orange come and go, giving and taking messages from Inspector Khan.

An air ambulance hovers over the mountain for a while.

"Goodness," says Gethin's mum. "Exciting," and then she looks as if she wishes she hadn't said it and goes back to herding the little ones.

Inspector Khan beeps and goes outside to talk into a walkie-talkie. He looks very serious when he comes back in. "Peter Romero has been found. The mountain rescue have him. They're bringing him here. He was in the quarry. But he's sustained gunshot wounds."

"Oh," I don't know what else to say. "Will he be OK?"

Inspector Khan shrugs, and picks cat hair from his trouser legs. "We hope so. Listen, there's something you ought to know. About his job—"

"Art recovery?" I ask.

The inspector shakes his head from side to side.

"Not strictly," he says.

"Is he a policeman?"

"Sort of…"

"MI something?"

"I never said that," he smiles.

"Vermeer?" I say.

He nods.

"Did you know that all the time?"

"No – we didn't," he replies. "Not until last night. He was so deep undercover that we assumed he was one of the gang."

"What are you two talking about?" asks Auntie V.

"Oh, nothing," says the inspector, removing a curl of cheese from his shoelaces.

His phone begins to buzz. "Yes," he says, standing. He glances across at me. "I suppose so."

He walks to the shattered window. "I see you. We'll be out in just a minute."

"Maya," he jerks his head towards the door. "Come with me, please."

# Chapter 29

I follow the inspector over the snow. My borrowed outsized boots are doing better than his expensive London brogues and I feel a snap of smugness. We stop next to an ambulance. A collection of people in hi-vis jackets and huge boots part as we approach and I see that in the middle is a man on a stretcher.

"Peter Romero?" is all I can think to say as we approach.

He's lying slightly propped, strapped down and with a bag of clear stuff piped into his arm. The white snowsuit is torn and bloody, and there's a huge rosette of crimson across his shoulder. He looks broken.

I don't feel that I should go anywhere near, but Helen appears at my elbow and propels me closer.

"This is Maya," she says, as if my dark skin and white streak weren't enough of a clue.

"Hi!" I say. "You're Peter Romero."

He turns his head. His face is almost as white as the snow, which makes his red hair redder and his blue eyes brighter. "I owe you an explanation," he says. His voice is Scottish. Of course I knew that, but somehow it makes him seem softer.

"Make it quick," says one of the mountain-rescue team. "We need to get you in the helicopter – don't want you dying here." They all laugh, but someone adjusts the drip and someone else jams more green things that look like hand towels from the school toilets on to his chest to absorb the blood.

Peter Romero ignores them. "I need to apologise."

"Why?" I say.

"For landing you in all of this – and for telling her you had the painting."

"Yeah – what was that about? She nearly killed Ollie."

Peter Romero bites his lip. "Sorry – but you

237

were the perfect excuse – the perfect way to get her to give herself away."

"I don't understand."

"You saw me, I saw you, but she saw you too. At first I just wanted to warn you about her. You were easy to find, with your white streak and your school uniform, and I knew she'd come after you because you had seen her there, with the gun."

"I thought it was you that had the gun?"

"It was her that pulled it. We'd planned a handover – she'd give me the painting, I'd give her the money. But she tried to double-cross me, we fought over the gun, but it was too dangerous there in the street, so I grabbed the painting and ran."

"I saw you run," I say.

"And then I found she'd killed my brother."

"She was the one who killed him?" interrupts Inspector Khan. "Why did she do that?"

"Her or one of her meatheads. She knew Georgio's heart wasn't in it. He wasn't really a thief, he was really an art historian." Romero goes quiet and looks at the pile of bloody handtowels on his chest. The inspector and I wait. "And I knew I needed to draw her out, that the promise of getting the painting back would be too tempting for her to resist. I needed to tell her that a third party had it, a soft target. I'm sorry, but you were that soft target."

"What? But I haven't got it."

Romero coughs and I don't know if it's because of the pain or because he's embarrassed. "Actually, you do. I put it in your bag when you were down by the river, the day they found Georgio's body. I sat next to you and your sister on a bench."

I'm almost speechless. "But – I mean surely I'd have found it?"

Inspector Khan starts texting someone from his phone.

"It's tiny, just a roll. I took it off the frame, and rolled it. I slipped it in the front pocket of your bag. You'd think it was a pencil. I knew you were under police observation the whole time. It was the safest place I could think of. I thought she'd shoot me next. You'd have found it in the end."

"Why didn't you tell us?" asks the inspector. "We could have retrieved it."

Romero sinks deeper on to the stretcher and his face tightens with pain. He ought to go to a hospital or somewhere but I want to know everything.

"I shouldn't have done it. It was stupid," he says.

"But I needed her out in the open. I've worked on this for years and I knew the painting would be irresistible."

"But I took it to school and everything." I imagine my bag swinging through the corridors, me sitting on it – all of that stuff. "I might have trashed it."

"It's in a fireproof plastic tube. It's practically indestructible." He pauses. "I wanted her to come after you at the farmhouse, I was going to get her then."

An incoherent bubble of fury builds in my chest.

I stare down at Peter Romero, bleeding on a stretcher.

"You used me as bait?"

"Yes," he says. "But it didn't go as I thought. I got arrested instead."

And suddenly I'm furious. "I could have been killed, my sister could have been killed! Ollie's still missing! And all over a stupid—"

I raise my arm to hit him, but the inspector stops me.

"Maya—" says Romero.

"We need to take you off now," interrupts a woman in a green jacket. "Sorry – you'll have to come to Birmingham if you need to talk further."

"Of course," says Inspector Khan, stepping back from the trolley as one of the paramedics slaps another dressing on the wound.

"Is it still there?" I shout, as a man in an orange jacket shoos me away. "The painting?"

But Peter Romero doesn't answer.

*  *  *

We retreat to the house, watching through a helicopter-induced blizzard as the stretcher is loaded in. The helicopter takes off straightaway.

As it sails up into the grey sky, I'm just thinking it could have spent a couple of minutes looking for Ollie when the door bursts open. Megan leaps from the ground as Ollie, wrapped in a silver emergency blanket, charges in through the door and throws himself on to the sofa. "I see you've eaten all the sandwiches," he says.

*  *  *

"I hid in an abandoned mine until the snow and the gunshots stopped."

"With an entire mountain-rescue force looking for you?" says Auntie V.

"I know, but I'm good at hide-and-seek."

Auntie V cuffs him over the back of his head.

"And then, later on, I heard the helicopters," says

Ollie. "And thought I'd better come out."

Auntie V hugs him for about the millionth time and Gethin's mum offers us more food.

Inspector Khan stands up and brushes cat hair and biscuit crumbs from his suit. "Good," he says. I suspect he finds family stuff odd. He doesn't look like a family man. He looks more like a catching murderers sort of a man.

Auntie V's still clutching Ollie when her phone goes off in her pocket.

"Sarah – yes – today? That's brilliant! But I haven't got any food in." Auntie V glances anxiously around the room as if it might suddenly turn into a supermarket. "You can? But that's great – and what about Dad?"

There's a long silence while I realise that Mum must be talking about Granddad.

Auntie V turns her back and walks to the window.

"OK – well, if you think he's well enough. I mean, the house is freezing."

And then I hear Mum saying loud and clear, "Well, do you *want* us to come down? We can always stay away, you know."

"Of course I want you – I've never wanted... We can light the fires in the bedrooms. It's just the

242

house is a bit – basic."

Another pause.

"Yes … yes … yes … brilliant," says Auntie V.

She finishes the call, sniffs and turns around.

"They're coming. They're all coming."

"Even Granddad?" I say.

Auntie V nods, her eyes are full of tears. "They're coming to our house for Christmas."

# Chapter 30

The stables smell awful when we get back, old kippers and singed wood and even though the snow fell heavily after the fire, there's still straw smouldering. A fire-investigation unit is poking about in the embers and emergency vehicles are scattered up the hillside, searching for evidence. Now in sunlight, I can see the car that we sent over the edge is halfway down the bracken slope, the one that the bulldozer tipped seems to have gone altogether, but the bulldozer is still up there on the track, dusted with snow.

"Bit different from yesterday morning?" says

Auntie V.

"I'm so sorry," I say.

She ruffles my hair in answer, picking up a horseshoe from the edge of the ash. She places it U-shaped against the porch. "To catch the luck," she says.

"How are the ponies?" asks Ollie.

The ponies in the garden have eaten everything they can get their teeth on – they're all there apart from the two we rode up the mountain. And they all look perfectly well. Ollie and I chase them into a windy cowshed at the back of the garden and bung hay in the mangers.

We watch them for a moment.

"They'll be OK when the snow melts," he says.

"Samson was brilliant on the mountain," I say. "He saved my life. And Megan – she showed me the way to the village."

"You'd never have made it you know," says Ollie. "Without them."

"I know," I say.

\* \* \*

The house seems fine. The power's restored. The dogs bark madly and snuffle about waiting to be fed.

I run up the stairs to find my bag still hanging on the door. Ollie follows.

"Seriously – in there?" he says. "With all your make-up and yuk?"

I tip the bag up and empty the whole thing on the bed.

We go through every last lipstick, search every pocket.

"It's not there," I say. "Perhaps—"

Ollie picks it up and shakes it really hard. A slim white biro thing slips from the front pocket and bounces on the eiderdown.

"Whoa!" he says. "Is that it?"

I pick it up and twirl it between my fingers. "I don't recognise it. I'm pretty sure I've never seen it before."

We look at each other. We look at the tube.

"Two hundred million," I say. "Can you believe it?"

"Well, open it," he says. "Let's have a look."

The end has a tiny white plug sealing it, and I try to get my nail underneath. It's really stiff.

Downstairs, someone bangs on the door, and Auntie V lets them in.

"Here, let me have a go," says Ollie, taking it off

me. He grabs the tube and locks the plug between his molars.

Feet sound on the stairs.

"Sorry," says someone behind me. I turn. It's Inspector Khan. He leans over the bed and grabs the tube from Ollie. "I'll take that."

"No! Can't we just—! Couldn't you show us?"

"No," says the inspector, hiding it in his jacket pocket. "You absolutely can't. No one but a restoration specialist should take it out of the tube. Certainly not you two."

"Aw!" sighs Ollie. "After all that – I really hoped we'd get to see it."

"Well, you got to hold it," replies the inspector.

"Kids," calls Auntie V from downstairs. "We need to get this house ready – it's a tip."

\* \* \*

I don't know where we get the energy from but while Ollie and Auntie V move around the house like slow zombies tidying and vacuuming and lighting fires – I go into full party mode. Firstly I find my inner Zahra – sourcing fairy lights, vases that I can put red berried holly in and things to make paper chains from. Poor Ollie then sits there cutting strips and we make a giant paper chain that stretches all around the inside of the house. I find some plastic flowers, wash them, and bung them in jam jars and plump all the cushions on the sofa. We cut a small pine from the side of the track, wedge it in a bucket and bring it inside as a Christmas tree. Auntie V nearly blows herself up resurrecting the fairy lights, and excels herself by producing a box of mangy Christmas decorations.

By four o'clock, the house is warm and looks pretty good and we eat Sergeant Lewis's leftover curry, this time with an appetite.

By five, we're all asleep on sofas.

"Hello, hello, hello!" Dad's voice booms in the hall. "Where are we at? Deck the hall and that! Merry Christmas to one and all!"

It's great, it's like having a bear come in. A huge cuddly magnificent strong bear – the whole family as one creature, all except Mum who just bursts into tears and drips all over me, and can't stop saying things like "so glad," and "so awful!" and hugging Auntie V and me, and even Ollie. Zahra glues herself to my side, hugging, and grinning and making stupid remarks that make me laugh. The twins race into the house and run round and round and pat the dogs who sniff at them and lick their faces.

And Granddad is standing there, looking really old but with this huge fabulous smile on his face, beaming at me, at Ollie and Auntie V.

Mum and Auntie V hug, streaming with tears, holding each other's hands – like sisters do.

And everyone's smiling and laughing and it feels really good.

"Oh, my lovely girl," says Mum, over and over. "My lovely girls, and she scoops Zahra to her side and holds us like she'll never let go and Auntie V holds us close on the other side and much to my surprise, Ollie joins in too.

* * *

On Christmas Day, Ollie brings the bulldozer down.

"Goodness gracious!" says Granddad, tiptoeing birdlike across the mud. "What a beauty she is. Can I have a go?"

So Christmas divides into two groups. Those playing bulldozers in the yard, and those playing Monopoly inside. It's a weird Christmas, with mismatched supermarket ready-meals and no presents, unless you count the rice krispy cakes that Zahra makes on Christmas morning.

But we eat together, and sing together, and laugh together.

\* \* \*

We stay until the day after Boxing Day, when Dad starts to get itchy feet and says that we really ought to go because: "The lads'll be after their U-bends."

In the morning, I go with Ollie and Megan for a last ride up the mountain. I take a pony called Duchess who doesn't bite and doesn't like liquorice. The snow has almost melted away – the grass is yellow underneath, with long scores where the bulldozer's tracks mashed the ground.

Megan races off, chasing imaginary crows.

"I didn't think I'd say this, but I'm going to miss it," I say.

"I didn't think I'd say it, but I'm going to miss you," Ollie says, and we trot up to the mine and he tells me that the bird that circles is a red kite and that he'd love it if I came back in the summer.

"Really, do you mean that?"

"Really," he says, "I really do."

# Epilogue

In May, just after my birthday, which was a proper party with Zahra and my friends and treats from Borough Market, a beautifully addressed envelope comes for all of us.

"What's in it?" asks Zahra.

"It's an invitation, to a private view. What's a private view?"

Granddad takes it and reads it. "It's your picture, sweetheart. The Vermeer. At Buckingham Palace."

"Picture, picture, picture!" shouts Precious, scribbling on the fridge.

* * *

We all go, even the twins. Ollie and Auntie V join us and we hold hands through the giant doorway and through all the posh people with fizzy wine and canapés.

Inspector Khan meets us, shaking hands with everyone and propelling us past the crowd to a smaller room on the side.

In the middle is a single painting on an easel. But no one seems to be looking at it – they're all just talking to each other, sipping from their sparkly wine glasses.

"Is that *it*?" says Zahra. "It's tiny."

"It is, isn't it?" says a voice from behind us. I turn, and face the buttons on a neat black suit. "Peter Romero, at your service." He looks utterly smart, not at all like the man I saw lying on the stretcher, and he doesn't have any bullet wounds, or blood. I almost wouldn't recognise him but for his flaming-red hair that catches in the powerful lights of the gallery like a halo, and his warm voice that echoes around the space.

"Hello," I say. "This is my sister, Zahra, and this is Ollie."

He shakes hands with his left hand and I realise that his right hand is tucked into his jacket. Perhaps he hasn't recovered yet.

"What do you think of the painting?" he asks.

Zahra wrinkles up her nose. "Is that all it is?"

It is tiny. It's a very small portrait of two girls holding hands. Behind them, more figures stand in near darkness in a corridor, but it's just possible to make out faces, smiling.

"It's lovely," says Mum. "It's really pretty. Warm. Loving."

"It's so fresh," says Auntie V. "It doesn't look like it was painted over three hundred years ago. It looks like it was done yesterday."

"Two hundred million dollars," says Dad. "For that."

"Wow," says Ollie.

"It's a very valuable painting. There aren't very many authenticated Vermeers in the world," says Peter Romero. "It's crazily rare. It's great to see it back where it belongs."

"Forget the money," says Granddad. "Look at the craftsmanship. Look at the light, the shade, the way it's painted. Beautiful."

"Look at the love there," says Auntie V.

I gaze at the faces of the two girls. One older, looking across at the younger one, her face full of warmth, and the little one smiling, bursting with energy.

They look really happy and so do the people behind them.

"They're just like us," I say.

"Yes," says Granddad, putting his arms around Ollie and me and Zahra. "They are."